3108

ACM 0314

mg/tc

A MAN WITH
NOWHERE TO GO

Tom Price recovers from a coma to find his life completely shattered. His daughter, Shelley, has gone away to college, his job no longer exists, and his wife loves someone else. He goes to Australia to convalesce and while there visits the widow of his associate killed in the car crash which injured him. Lisa and her family are struggling for survival on a drought-stricken cattle station in the Outback. Concealing his true identity, Tom stays to help . . .

Books by Sheila Lewis
in the Linford Romance Library:

FOR LOVE OF LUCIA
DESTROY NOT THE DREAM
A PROMISE FOR TOMORROW
KENNY, COME HOME
STARS IN HER EYES

SHEILA LEWIS

A MAN WITH NOWHERE TO GO

Complete and Unabridged

LINFORD
Leicester

First published in Great Britain in 1985 by
Robert Hale Limited
London

First Linford Edition
published 2002
by arrangement with
Robert Hale Limited
London

British Library CIP Data

Lewis, Sheila
    A man with nowhere to go.—
    Large print ed.—
    Linford romance library
    1. Love stories
    2. Large type books
    I. Title
    823.9′14 [F]

    ISBN 0–7089–9942–5

Published by
F. A. Thorpe (Publishing)
Anstey, Leicestershire

Set by Words & Graphics Ltd.
Anstey, Leicestershire
Printed and bound in Great Britain by
T. J. International Ltd., Padstow, Cornwall

This book is printed on acid-free paper

1

At first there was just a sensation of light, murmurs of sound, suggestions of movement. But Tom Price could not find the strength to define anything. Sleep was a cocoon of comfort. Then, after a while — an hour, a day, a week? — curiosity to identify the comforting hands, and the necessity for them, finally penetrated the haze of half sleep.

'Hello, Mr Price, are you awake now?'

A strange voice. He concentrated. A nurse. White walls. A hospital. Why? He couldn't remember.

Next time he woke Joyce was sitting by his bed. Again he needed concentration. Yes, it was Joyce, his wife . . . and yet, she seemed different in some way.

It was she who told him about the accident. A car accident. He listened to her, but it meant nothing. After she'd

1

gone home, he tried to think. He'd been going to Leeds that day, Joyce said. Why Leeds? He had no idea, no recollection. But it had been cold. Yes, he remembered that! The car windows had been misty. Fog perhaps? He'd run slap into the back of a lorry, so the police had told Joyce. He couldn't remember that part. Just as well, perhaps. He stirred uneasily in the crisp sheets.

At once a nurse materialized by his bedside. How had she known to come so quickly? Had she been sitting by his bed?

'Headache, Mr Price? Don't worry, we'll soon fix that,' he heard her say.

How had she known? He smiled slightly at her. It was a corker of a headache all right. He eased his long body down the bed. Strange that, he had no other pain, no splints, no dressings. Nothing. Surely he hadn't escaped that easily? He must have hit the driving wheel with terrific force. Gingerly he ran his hand across his chest. Ribs felt okay, no bandages.

His gaze drifted towards the window. Outside the sky was clear, no sign of fog, or even mist today. There was a vase of flowers on the window-sill, dahlias and sweet peas. He wondered if Joyce had brought these from the garden. Was it summer then? But it had been cold in the car. Very cold.

The nurse came back with some medication.

His 'Thank you' was difficult to say. He couldn't speak very well. Another girl in a white coat had been in to see him earlier, saying she was a speech therapist. Why did he need her services?

When Joyce visited him next evening, he saw what was different about her. It was her hair, caught back in a thick French pleat. He last remembered her hair short, a dark brown cap for her head.

He pointed at her head. 'Hair . . . different.'

'Yes, Tom. It's . . . been a long time.'

He stared at her uncomprehendingly. 'You've been unconscious.'

He nodded. So that was it.

'In a coma, Tom. For . . . for eighteen months.'

He felt cold again. Very cold. He shook his head at Joyce, then turned away and closed his eyes.

She was back again the next evening to visit him. A whole twenty-four hours had passed but he still couldn't accept that he'd been lying on this bed for a year and a half. Eighteen months out of his life. It couldn't be possible. Joyce must be mistaken.

She was watching him anxiously, as if she knew he couldn't believe what she'd told him.

'Shelley is coming to see you tomorrow evening, Tom,' she told him.

Shelley! His beloved only child.

Joyce read the question in his eyes. 'She's fine. Doing so well. Longing to see you again.'

She laid a hand on his arm.

'I asked her to wait until you'd come

4

round completely. I thought you'd want that, too, Tom.'

He nodded. Yes, that was sensible of Joyce. He didn't want to frighten Shelley, lying like this.

'Only my head hurts now,' he managed to say.

'Yes, everything else has healed with time,' Joyce spoke quietly. She took her hand away.

That's the first time she's touched me, Tom thought irrationally. Oh, perhaps he was wrong. He might have forgotten. He sometimes couldn't even remember what he'd had for lunch an hour later. Everything was still so confused.

'Shelley passed all her exams, took her A-levels.'

He gripped the sheet. He couldn't quite cope with all this yet. He felt as if he was hurtling through time. He had to come to terms with the fact that eighteen months had virtually disappeared out of his life. Out of his life with Joyce and Shelley. He'd missed all that time with his family. The sense of loss was frightening, terrifying even.

'I'll go home now, Tom, let you rest,' Joyce said. He knew she could see his distress.

'Don't worry about a thing. Shelley and I have coped — and now you're going to be all right.'

Next day the doctor gave him the facts about the extent of his injuries. He realized he was lucky to be alive. Joyce had been a daily visitor to his bedside. The strain on her must have been terrific. But then Joyce had always been so loyal, so loving. Shelley had visited him, too, as often as the doctors would permit. His throat felt tight as he thought of all those months they had visited him here in hospital, not knowing if he would live or not.

He both longed for and dreaded the next day. Longed to see his beloved only child again, yet dreaded what changes he might see in her. He slept badly, could hardly eat breakfast and was restless when the nurses shaved him. At last visiting time arrived.

She came into his room hesitantly, a little line of tension on her forehead.

'Hi, Dad,' her voice was a little shaky. As was his. 'Hello . . . my love.'

'I'm glad you're . . . you're better. Oh, Dad!' She knelt by the bed and her head came down on the pillow beside his. She was weeping tears, tears that had been pent up for eighteen months.

With a trembling hand, he stroked the soft hair, fighting tears himself. He might never have seen her again.

Then he lifted his eyes and saw Joyce standing watching then, smiling gently. Tom could only nod to her, speech was impossible. He stretched out a hand to her. She took it, still smiling, but she wasn't crying. Maybe her tears were all spent months ago.

Gradually the days became longer as he slept less. He was impatient to be out of hospital, but he had to take things slowly. The physiotherapist worked hard with him, but he had to learn to use all his muscles again.

Sitting up was a milestone, feeding himself another. Learning to walk again was a revelation. No longer would he take his body for granted.

But his mind was racing ahead of his body. He began to think about his business. How had his partner, Alan Markham, coped with things for a year and a half? Building was not a business that could be suspended for a time. People were waiting for houses to be completed.

Joyce had been evasive when he'd asked about the office. Either she was trying not to worry him, or she didn't know anything. But now he was ready for some facts and asked her on her next visit.

'Well, this will come as a big surprise, Tom,' she began a little nervously. 'But I've been helping out at the office. Oh, just paper work and phone calls at first to help Alan — he missed you dreadfully and just couldn't cope alone. Then, after a few months we decided — Alan insisted that I had a vote in it

8

— that he should take over as Managing Director. You still have all your shares and the income from them, of course, and Alan has done marvellously, just as you would have done. The business is bigger than ever,' she stopped, a little breathlessly.

He said nothing, it was all a bit too much to take in.

'Don't be too upset, Tom, it seemed the only course at the time,' she was watching him anxiously.

He nodded. 'Yes, I quite agree. The only course,' he caught her anxious look. 'I approve, Joyce, really.'

Quickly she told him of new developments, projected plans.

'You're still helping out?'

There was a brief pause, then she answered. 'Well, yes. I was really needed and it helped to fill in the days, Tom. But now — it's a real job. With me being in the office, Alan can get out round the sites and attend meetings. To tell the truth, Tom, I'd forgotten what it was like to work so hard!'

'Good for you, you've been marvellous, my love,' Tom told her.

She flushed and looked away. 'Oh well, I felt I was doing *something*, helping. Knowing, or at least thinking, that's what you would have wanted me to do.'

He grinned. 'Sure, keeping my old job open for me — that's my girl.'

The anxious look came back to her face. 'You've a long way to go, Tom, before you are fit for work again.'

'Just you wait,' he told her.

A few days later Alan came to visit him. A couple of years younger than Tom, Alan was one of those men who seem to improve as the years go by. He was still slim, carrying his six-foot frame without a stoop and the touches of grey in his hair were attractive, not ageing.

'Look like a blooming film star, you do,' Tom teased him.

Alan shrugged, smiling slightly. 'Well, I've been lucky.'

'I'll soon be back, fighting fit and all

that. You'll have to watch out then,' Tom said.

'I bought that piece of land near Leeds,' Alan said quickly. 'Went up the next day after your accident. Just made the deadline.'

'Oh, really?' So that's why he'd been going to Leeds!

'What did you build there?'

'The Georgian style villas. Gone like a bomb. Could have sold each one four times over. Developed the other areas we planned, too.'

'Oh?' If only he could remember more details, more facts.

Alan gave him a detailed outline of the business progression. Tom was amazed at the developments there had been in eighteen months.

'Things are going so well, Tom, that your income is quite something now. You won't have any financial problems in the future, I can assure you of that. You can put your feet up for the rest of your life.'

Tom stared at him. 'That just what I

don't want to do. I want to get back in harness again. Now, where can you fit me in?'

'Hey, hang about, we've got to get you well again. Plenty of time to discuss matters then.'

Tom lay back on his pillows. He was grateful to Alan for looking after the business so well and being so considerate of his well-being. He put the business out of his mind.

'And what about yourself, Alan? How have you been this last year and a half. Found anyone special yet?' Tom knew Alan had been lonely since his wife had died some years ago.

Alan took a cigarette from his case, lit it, then suddenly looked round.

'I forgot. Mustn't smoke in here. Sorry, Tom. Me? Oh, I've been so busy, you know. Which reminds me, must dash, got an appointment with the County Surveyor,' he got up. 'Besides, I can finish my cigarette outside. See you, me old mate,' and he was gone.

Tom felt rather let down after Alan

left. Business was booming, money was no problem, but he'd have liked to know exactly what job Alan had in mind for him. Obviously Alan was enjoying the command and he wouldn't take that away from him, but —

Of course, Alan wasn't sure how competent he would be after the accident. Well, he could understand that. It was up to him to get himself back to normal. Show them he was capable of anything . . . of everything.

★ ★ ★

At last the day came when he was ready to leave hospital. Joyce came in the car for him and he walked down the hospital steps with the Sister who'd looked after him for the whole eighteen months.

'Our reward is seeing our patients leave us,' she told him as he thanked her gratefully.

The first thing he saw when Joyce drove into the drive was a huge

'*Welcome Home, Dad*' banner across the front door.

He was almost bowled over by Shelley's exhuberant hug. Inside, the house was festooned with balloons and streamers.

'Hey, it's just like Christmas!' he cried.

'Of course,' said Shelley. 'This is the one you missed. I've even cooked you a Christmas dinner.'

'In summer? Crazy child, adorable child . . . my girl,' he kissed the soft cheek.

'Not so much of a child, my man,' Shelley said with mock severity. 'Your daughter is about to embark on a college course in hotel management.'

'You passed all your exams then?' Tom said slowly, knowing this to be the case, but still hardly able to accept the fact that his little girl was about to step into the adult world.

'Being your daughter, I wouldn't have dared otherwise,' she teased him.

Shelley had cooked the full Christmas dinner, all by herself. Tom had to admit that it was delicious even though he could not eat much of it. Then there were the presents they'd bought for him last Christmas.

'You bought these for me — not knowing?' he asked, as he slowly unwrapped the packages.

'Shelley never gave up,' Joyce said quietly. 'She never lost hope for you.'

Tom hid his eyes as he stared unseeingly at his gifts. He wondered if Shelley's faith had helped pull him through.

'By the way, Dad, you bought me a tape recorder last Christmas. I like it a lot. Thanks a bunch,' said the irrepressible Shelley.

He looked at his grinning daughter. 'Don't mention it, it was a pleasure. I guess I have a couple of your birthdays to catch up on.'

'You sure do, but I'm working on those.'

After dinner, Joyce and Shelley disappeared to the kitchen to do the washing up. They wouldn't let him help at all. He didn't protest. He was glad of a quiet doze.

'Hey, this is a party,' he woke to hear Shelley speaking to him.

'Dad mustn't overdo things, dear,' Joyce told her. 'He has to take it easy at first. In fact, Tom, I don't want to be a wet blanket but I think an early bed is in order for you tonight.'

He made a rueful face, but was quietly glad that Joyce had given him the excuse, he was exhausted.

'Sorry to spoil your party, pet,' he put an arm round Shelley's shoulder.

'Not much of a party when the star guest leaves, but I guess you do need some beauty sleep,' she kissed his cheek. 'Actually . . . I was due to play in a tennis tournament tonight but I backed out — '

'Then back right in again. Go on, knock 'em for six,' he told her.

'Actually, that's cricket, Dad, but I think I get your drift.' She kissed him again and turned to Joyce.

'Is it okay if I take the car? Derek will

have left by now.'

'Take the car?' Tom looked at her in amazement. 'But you've only got your provisional licence.'

There was a short silence.

'Not any longer, Dad,' Shelley said gently. 'I passed my test.'

Of course, he was eighteen months out of date!

'Who gave you lessons when I wasn't here?'

Again Shelley hesitated. 'Alan did.'

'Ah . . . of course. And who is Derek?'

'He's my boyfriend.'

'You'll like him, Tom,' Joyce said. 'He's a nice boy.'

'If your mum approves then it's fine by me,' Tom told his daughter.

'See you,' she kissed her parents and was gone.

'The car — she will be careful?' he looked at Joyce.

'Yes, of course. She's very competent, just like you, Tom.'

Competent! After an accident like

he'd had! He felt the tight band of the recurring headache assault him again.

'I'm bushed, Joyce. I'd better go upstairs.'

She followed him and they went into their bedroom. Quickly she turned down the covers on the bed. Tom looked a little uncomprehendingly at the single pillow on the bed.

'I thought,' Joyce's voice was a little more highly pitched than usual, 'that — that I'd use the spare room. You still need quiet, the doctor said. I don't want to disturb you in any way.'

'Yes, of course,' he said mechanically. 'That's . . . considerate of you.' He turned towards her, but somehow they could not look at each other.

'Doctor Stevenson said you would need to be very careful,' she said, drawing the curtains. 'Now you slip into bed and I'll fetch some cocoa.'

She brought cocoa and biscuits, magazines and a book, a glass of water and a bell to ring if he needed her during the night. She tidied his clothes away, straightened up the bed, plumped his pillows, and then with a quiet 'Good night, sleep well' she left the bedroom.

Tom sank onto the bed and looked at that lonely pillow. He did need something — someone — his wife. He knew it would be a little while yet before he could be the husband he had once been to Joyce, but he'd been longing so much just to lie beside her, to know she was *there*, with him, to be aware of the warmth of her body, to have physical contact with her, no matter how slight.

Perhaps he was being unfair to Joyce. She was being considerate. Yet if only she'd stayed here in the room with him for half an hour or so, it would have meant so much.

Exhaustion brought sleep, but he was restless all night.

When Shelley brought him breakfast in bed next morning he sat up and glanced at the bedside clock in amazement.

'Good grief, Shelley. It's only seven-thirty. Have you turned over a new leaf or is your alarm two hours fast?'

'Ha ha, very funny.' Expertly she sliced the top off his boiled egg. 'I'm a working girl at the moment, doing my waitress bit at the Golf Club until the college term begins.'

Later, Joyce came in with the morning paper and sat on the edge of the bed, chatting about neighbours and friends. He noticed she was wearing a smart suit, not the usual slacks and shirt she donned for housework.

'What about the job, Joyce?' he asked.

'Well,' she twisted her hands a little nervously. 'We certainly are very busy at the moment with tenders for a new council contract, but I didn't want to leave you on your own all day, so I thought I'd only do part-time until you're really up and about.'

He smiled at her. 'That was very thoughtful. But look, I'm going to have to rest a bit at first and I won't be much company for you, so why don't you make sure my job's still safe.' He squeezed her hand. 'Go and keep my office chair warm for me.'

She jumped up. 'If you're really sure, Tom . . . there's so much to do.'

Before she left, Joyce told him that she now had a daily woman, a Mrs Burrows, and that she'd left a note asking her to make lunch for him.

When she'd gone, Tom read the paper, but some of the big issues were utterly meaningless to him. Obviously he had a lot to catch up on. He showered and shaved, then went downstairs. The house was immaculately clean, quiet, still. There was nothing to do. He looked out of the window. There was nowhere he could go.

The days passed, with the same pattern being repeated without variation. Mrs Burrows was pleasant enough, but only interested in doing the housework and shooting off to her home again.

Tom found that the only person he

could really talk to was Frank Stevenson, his doctor.

'Sometimes I wish I was back in hospital,' he blurted out to him one day.

'It's not as bad as that, surely, Tom. Look, you've got a bit of adjusting to do. I'll let you back to work as soon as I think you're fit. Not before.'

Frank packed the stethoscope back in his case.

'I feel as if I've been away eighteen years, not eighteen months,' Tom said. 'I feel . . . like a stranger to my family. I can't explain it.'

Frank Stevenson sat down again. 'Joyce and Shelley have a great deal of psychological adjusting to do as well as you, Tom. Nobody really expected you to pull through, especially as time went on. Joyce has made, not a new life, but a different one. Things will work out all right — give them time. Now how about a holiday?' he finished bracingly.

'A holiday? Go away again when I've just come home after eighteen months?' Tom swung round on the doctor. 'I want to get back to work.'

'All in good time,' the doctor promised.

With little to do all day, Tom found he was brooding over the car accident. He still could remember very little of it and Joyce had been unable to help.

'I don't remember all the details now, Tom,' she said when he asked. 'It's a long time ago. Forget it — it's in the past. You've come through it.'

But he *wanted* to know everything about that day. He knew there had been fog on the motorway and therefore the crash must have happened very suddenly. Naturally, he would remember nothing after that. But why had he been going to look at a site in Leeds anyway? That was usually Alan's job.

'Oh, he was busy that day, or something,' was Joyce's vague answer.

Frank Stevenson had warned him that occasional lapses of memory were the result of his long spell of unconsciousness, but he was determined to fit together all the pieces of the jigsaw picture of that day.

With the help of his road maps, he studied the route he must have taken from the office to Leeds. He read aloud the names of the various places he must have passed en route. There — his finger jabbed the map — that was where he'd mentioned the fog warning lights on the motorway. He remembered that quite distinctly.

His finger froze on the map. Mentioned? Mentioned to whom? Had there been someone with him in the car? Desperately he tried to penetrate the mists surrounding his memory. Slowly, gradually, the picture cleared. Yes . . . there had been someone . . . someone who wanted to visit Leeds. Someone who'd wanted to drive Tom's Rover, and who was unfamiliar with British roads.

Of course! It had been Bill Donnelly, the Australian! He'd been over in Britain picking up some pointers on setting up his own building business back home. Tall, rangy, just like Tom's idea of a typical Australian, Bill couldn't have been much over thirty, with a wife and two kids back home. His wife, Lisa, was worried about him being so far away and Bill could hardly wait to get home again.

But why had no one mentioned Bill? Why hadn't Joyce said anything about him? He'd asked her often enough about the accident. Had Bill been badly injured? After all, he'd been driving.

With awful, cold clarity a possible answer struck him. Joyce was barely in the door that evening before he asked her.

'What about Bill Donnelly? What happened to him? You've never mentioned him. Was he badly hurt? Is he back home in Australia now?'

She carefully put her bag on the hall table. The delaying tactic told him everything.

'No, no,' he collapsed in the chair. 'He wasn't — '

'Yes, Tom, I'm sorry,' Joyce's voice was gentle. 'He was killed outright. In one way he was luckier than you, he suffered nothing.'

'Luckier? Joyce, there was a wife and two kids out there, waiting for him, living for him. What about them?'

'I don't know. I can't say. Alan wrote to her but we never had any reply.'

Bill Donnelly's death haunted him for days. The Australian had had a keen sense of humour and though their acquaintance had been brief, Tom felt they could have been good friends. There had even been a tentative invitation given by Bill for Tom and family to visit Australia. Tom had given it serious thought. After all, he'd one or two contacts on the Australian continent and the trip would have made a good holiday for them all.

Now all that was in the past. The far past. Eighteen months ago. A year and a half since Lisa Donnelly had been windowed. How had she coped? Had she enough money? Things might even have deteriorated as time went by. Bill might not have been insured. His wife might have found it necessary to find a job.

With little else to occupy his mind, the worries about Lisa Donnelly magnified themselves in Tom's mind until he realized he would have no peace unless he did something about her. But what? He could write to her. All he could offer was sympathy and money. Still, she might need both.

Once he'd made the decision to write, he was impatient to send the letter off. He searched through his desk, but could not find the Donnellys' address. It must be at the office. He stretched out his hand to dial the office phone number then he had a better idea. He'd go to the office himself!

He was much stronger now and although Dr Stevenson still considered him unfit for work, this would only be a visit. Besides, he would like to see the staff again, and see his old office, his familiar desk, sit in the swivel chair again. He was longing to get back to work.

He got up from his chair, full of enthusiasm. He had something to do and somewhere to go.

He ordered a taxi, then changed into his best suit. That was better, he was beginning to look a different man already.

Joyce had spoiled him since he had returned home, giving him every luxury, the best food, every comfort — except her nearness, the one thing he really wanted. It wasn't an easy thing to define, but he sensed they had somehow grown apart.

The taxi dropped him at the works' gate and immediately there was a heartening welcome from the gateman. Inside the yard, it was just the same. Tools were downed while men came over to speak to him, wiping dirty hands on overalls before shaking hands with him, or giving him a gentle slap across the shoulders.

There were also quite a number of men who looked at him with curiosity, but not acquaintance. Tom realized the work force had increased considerably in his absence.

Inside the office, the pattern was repeated. Hands were lifted from typewriters, heads raised from ledgers all to give him a greeting. Then it was back to work. Tom was amazed. Everyone was busy and it was clear that the company had gone from strength to strength. Someone looked in a file and gave him the Donnellys' address.

Joyce looked positively alarmed when he walked into her office.

'Hello, just felt like getting in the swim again,' he smiled at her.

'Do you think you should have come, Tom? Dr Stevenson — '

'Fussy old hen,' Tom joked, looking around. 'You've made this office very nice.'

It was actually his office. The walls had been re-papered and there was a softer, more elegant air about the room. It suited Joyce very well.

'I'll make some coffee, Tom, you look a bit tired.' She went to the automatic coffee maker sitting on a table in the corner of the room.

'I'm much better now, Joyce, almost back to normal.' He stressed the latter half of his sentence.

Joyce flushed, but did not reply.

'You've only put out two cups,' Tom said, watching her prepare a tray. 'Let's ask Alan to join us.'

'I don't think he's in,' she said quickly.

'I'll soon find out,' Tom lifted the internal telephone receiver and dialled Alan's number. 'I haven't seen him since he came to visit me in hospital anyway.' And that was only once, he reflected. Alan hadn't visited him at home at all.

'Line's engaged. I'll slip along to his office.'

He strode out of Joyce's room and along the corridor. The familiarity of the works office was comforting and challenging at the same time. This was exactly what he needed to get the old adrenalin flowing again. This was the best aid to recovery. He'd have to tell Frank Stevenson that!

Alan was just replacing the receiver when Tom entered his office.

'Tom! I had no idea you were coming in today. Joyce said nothing — '

'She didn't know. I didn't know. Sudden impulse!' He walked over to Alan's desk and held out his hand.

Alan rose, a little uncertainly, and shook Tom's hand.

'Had to come in and congratulate the Managing Director.'

Alan looked uneasy. 'Look, Tom — '

Tom laughed. 'Hey, I meant it. You've done so well, and becoming M.D. was the only thing to do in the circumstances. I'm not here to stab you in the back.'

His former partner still looked ill-at-ease.

So this was why he hadn't visited him, Tom thought. He was embarrassed about being the head of the firm, usurping what might have been Tom's place.

'Look, Alan, I'm glad about this — '
he waved his hand round the director's
office. 'Come on — coffee in my, sorry,
Joyce's office.'

'Oh,' Alan fiddled with some pens on
his desk, 'thanks, but I don't — '

'Come on, surely you can spare me a
few minutes?'

Alan looked shamefaced for a moment,
then said briskly, 'Of course, Tom. I
don't know what I was thinking about.
It's . . . it's good to see you up and
about again.'

Together they walked along the
corridor. Tom was a little shorter than
Alan, and certainly a couple of stones
lighter. His suit was ill-fitting now, he
realized. He would have to buy some
new clothes before coming back to
work.

Joyce had the coffee ready and
handed each man a cup as soon as they
arrived. Tom looked at his wife and
business partner. He felt himself come
alive again. He was back in business
— well, almost, but his companions

didn't appear to share his zest.

'Well now let's get down to brass tacks. Where do I fit in?' Tom settled himself in the armchair and looked expectantly at the others.

They exchanged a brief look.

'Dr Stevenson — ' Joyce began.

'He isn't infallible. I know I'm ready to come back here.'

'You mustn't tax your strength,' Alan said quickly. 'You have plenty of money, you know, Tom. There's no need to wear yourself out at the daily grind.'

There was a short silence. 'You have kept a place for me, haven't you?' Tom asked quietly.

Again he noticed an exchange of looks.

'Well, actually — ' Alan looked embarrassed again, just as he had in his office, and suddenly it struck Tom that there could be another reason for it — that he didn't *want* him back in the firm. Was that why he hadn't been to visit him? Was that why Joyce had been trying to put him off coming to the office?

'You don't need me here, do you?' Unsteadily he got to his feet. 'You don't want me, do you?' He was shouting now, unable to control the shock and hurt he felt. There was no place for him here, even this office was no longer his. 'You two get along very nicely without me!'

Joyce turned to him. 'Oh, Tom, we didn't mean this to happen.'

Alan crossed to the window and looked out, as if unable to face Tom.

'We were working together and Alan was helping me in so many ways,' Joyce's voice was high as the words tumbled out. 'We never thought that it would . . . that we would feel this way about each . . . ,' her voice trailed off.

Tom swayed against the back of the chair. She wasn't talking about the business, about a job for him. She was talking about Alan . . . and herself!

The realization of what she meant galvanized him into action and he hurled himself towards the door to leave the office, but the sudden effort

34

was a shock to his still shaky system and almost at once the floor rushed up to meet him.

★ ★ ★

When he woke he was back in bed again. Dr Stevenson had said that it was a relapse, but it wasn't anything to worry about. It might happen once or twice before he was fully fit, especially if he was unwise enough to strain himself.

'That'll teach you to go back to work before you're ready,' he said to Tom.

Tom nodded. He didn't tell him the real reason for his adverse reaction. He simply hadn't suspected how things stood between Alan and Joyce. He'd only meant that Joyce and Alan couldn't find a job for him in the business again when he'd shouted at them. He'd never guessed that . . . that there was something between them. Joyce's revelation had almost paralysed him. No wonder he'd passed out.

Since that day she'd apologized again

and again. Oh, he knew they hadn't meant to fall in love and he knew things like that happened at times of crisis, but he needed and loved Joyce so much.

For Shelley's sake, he behaved as normally as possible. Last-minute preparations were now under way for the start of her college term and the whirl of activity kept her occupied and her mind elsewhere.

It wasn't until a few days before her departure that Tom realized he would see very little of her in future. She would only be able to come home for the occasional weekend as the college was over a hundred miles away. Life was reaching out to her and he couldn't stand in her way, no matter how much he needed her.

But he would have to find something to do, or he would crack up completely. The relapse had set him back a bit, and it wasn't yet possible for him to look for another job. Maybe Frank Stevenson's idea of a holiday was the best answer.

He remembered then about Lisa

Donnelly. He'd never posted that letter to her. Maybe he could take a couple of months' holiday in Australia; see her, square the situation, make sure that she and her children were not in need of anything. That would be one problem off his mind.

Besides, the trip would give him time to think, time to sort out his life. Maybe when he came back, he and Joyce could make a go of it again. After all, they'd had a good marriage — until the accident.

He'd lost eighteen months of his life — but he still had so much life to live. In the meantime, though, he'd have to go it alone . . .

2

The taxi driver kept up a running commentary to Tom Price as he drove him through the streets of Sydney.

Tom didn't hear much of what he said, although he enjoyed the warm tones of the man's Australian twang and the easy friendliness with which he was treated.

He was tired, so tired. When the taxi drew up outside a small hotel, he over-tipped the driver to make up for his inattention on the drive.

'There's a good bus tour round Sydney, you can see all the sights in comfort. I hope you enjoy your stay here,' the driver said.

Tom looked at the tanned, broad face. In a day or two, he would really enjoy this man's company.

'Maybe you would show me the sights. I could hire your taxi for a day,' he asked.

'Sure thing, nothing like a native to show you the real Sydney. Just ask for Steve at the Taxi office,' he said. 'Come on, I'll carry your bags into the hotel, you looked real pooped, mister.'

Tom was glad he'd made the hotel reservation from England as it only took a few minutes to register, send cables to Joyce and Shelley advising them of his safe arrival, and then he was able to escape to the quiet sanctuary of his bedroom.

It was a pleasant room, simply but attractively furnished with pine furniture. The walls were covered in a pale lemon-patterned paper, and the carpet, curtains and bed coverings were in sunny shades of yellow.

He asked the porter to send up some tea and sandwiches and, without even unpacking his tooth-brush, lay down on the bed. He could still hardly believe he was in Sydney, Australia, half way round the world from his home and wife and daughter. As he thought of Joyce and Shelley a sense of utter loneliness invaded him. He'd felt so lost, so bereft on the long air flight, that more than once at the various stops, he'd almost taken another flight back to Britain. Were they missing him, too?

Vividly he remembered Joyce's appalled reaction when he'd told her of his holiday plan.

'Australia? Whatever for, Tom?' Then her expression changed. 'It's to get away from me, isn't it, because I let you down? Because of Alan and me — '

'No, Joyce, it isn't, please calm down, please don't blame yourself for everything! I'm not hitting out at you.' He went quickly to the sideboard and poured a brandy for her.

'Here, take this and just let me speak.'

She took the balloon glass and moved to a chair, but she sat on it tensed like a bird about to take flight.

'I'm far from well yet, Joyce, and you are too overwrought at the moment to know what you really want,' he began, trying hard not to make a bald

40

statement about Joyce not knowing whether she wanted to stay married to him or to go to Alan Markham.

'If we have a time apart,' he went on, 'you'll be able to think things out without me walking round like a shadow on your thoughts. I'll be able to get fit again and then we'll both know exactly what's right for us,' he paused. 'And we can explain our decision to Shelley, whatever it is, knowing that we've thought it out rationally and sensibly.'

It was a calm speech which he had carefully rehearsed.

Joyce was silent for a bit. 'But Australia — why so far away?' she asked.

'It will be almost summer when I get there and I need sun, need a new place to interest me. I can also look up Bill Donnelly's widow and see that she's okay.' He made no mention of the fact that he also intended to contact an old friend, Norrie Hampson, who'd emigrated to Australia fifteen years ago.

Norrie was still in the building trade and just might be able to find Tom a job.

'I'm still not happy,' Joyce said.

He stretched out a hand to reassure her, then withdrew it again without touching her. Neither of them was emotionally ready for one of their familiar loving gestures.

'Look, Joyce, I'm not running away and you're not sending me away. It's a convalescent trip.'

He convinced her of the logic of his decision but he could see that it still bothered her. Maybe she was right, he thought now, maybe I've made things worse by coming so far from home.

His thoughts switched to Shelley. He'd made a special trip to her college to tell her about his holiday.

'What's wrong with Bournemouth?' had been her first, slightly jokey reaction.

'No kangaroos there,' Tom retaliated, but he'd seen the uncertainty in her eyes and he wondered, not for the first time, if she had any suspicions about the strained relationship between Joyce and himself.

'Shelley my love, if I decide to stay over Christmas, then I'll fly you and your mother out to join me. O.K.?'

His words had reassured her at the time, but both she and Joyce had been tearful at Heathrow airport and it had taken all his courage and determination to leave them.

Now he wanted more than anything to talk to them. He reached out for the phone to call home, then withdrew his hand abruptly. Was he being fair to Joyce? She was already feeling guilty and would soon detect the loneliness in his voice. He was no actor and wouldn't be able to disguise his feelings. Phoning Shelley would only worry her, too.

No, he'd made the decision, he'd better stick to it. One thing was sure, though, he'd be back in England for Christmas.

The tea and sandwiches arrived and he ate and drank a little, while glancing through 'The Sydney Morning Herald' which the porter had brought with him. But the newsprint danced before his eyes and he couldn't concentrate on anything.

He slept badly, more on account of his loneliness than jet lag, he reckoned. He decided to visit Norrie Hampson in the morning. He wanted someone familiar to talk to, if nothing else.

Norrie's office was on the tenth floor of an impressive building and it looked as if he'd done very well for himself, Tom thought. He looked out of the picture window that gave a magnificent view of Sydney, while the receptionist took his name into Norrie.

He straightened his tie and adjusted his cuffs. He'd bought some light-weight clothes suitable for the climate and he was wearing a smart two-piece grey suit which made him look a lot better. Yet he saw the shock in Norrie's eyes when he was ushered into his office. His old friend came round from behind his desk and walked over to greet Tom.

Norrie, a big man, still retained some of his ruddy Yorkshire colour.

'Well, me old mate,' he greeted Tom. 'What are you doing in this neck of the woods?'

Tom explained briefly that he'd bought out of his old company back home and was in Australia for a holiday.

'Going walkabout at your age?'

Tom smiled at the mixture of Yorkshire accent and Australian slang.

'Yes, exploring in a way,' he paused. 'Exploring the chances of finding a job here.'

'With me?' Norrie said with his usual forthrightness.

'If possible,' Tom was honest.

Norrie pointed to an armchair. 'Sit down and have a beer, best drink in any country,' he laughed.

Tom did as he was told, well aware that behind Norrie's banter, he was being assessed pretty thoroughly.

'Going to give it to me on the level?' Norrie asked, after they'd sat drinking for a few moments.

Tom replaced his glass on the low table by his chair, wondering just how much Norrie saw, or guessed.

'You don't look to me like a man who's just made a pile of money,' Norrie said. 'You look like a man who's carrying a hod-full of troubles.'

Tom took another swallow of beer, then faced Norrie.

'It was a road accident. I was unconscious for eighteen months.'

Norrie's glass hit the table with some force.

'Holy mackerel, Tom, you ought to be dead!'

'But I'm not. I will be though if I don't get something to do.'

Norrie stared at him for several seconds. 'I guess I'd feel the same way,' He got up and moved about the room. 'Things are different out here, you know, Tom.'

'Yes, I guessed they would be, but I still think — '

'Sure, sure,' Norrie spoke, just a little

too quickly. 'I haven't anything here at the moment, that is,' he said a little evasively, 'but of course I have contacts. Leave it with me Tom, I may be able to come up with something. May take a little time, of course. If you'd written first — '

'I didn't think — coming here was just a spur of the moment decision.' Tom got to his feet. He knew it was time to go.

'Call me in a week or so. Oh, heck, what am I thinking of, come and have dinner with Pat and me,' Norrie said. 'She'll be so happy to see you again. Make it Thursday. Here's my address.' He handed a business card to Tom.

As he left Norrie's office, Tom felt the onset of one of his headaches again. Dr Stevenson had told him to expect these and fatigue from time to time as part of the process of returning to health. He knew that today, however, disappointment was partly the reason for the headache. Norrie Hempson was just not prepared to take a chance on him, yet. He wandered around Sydney that afternoon, morose and unhappy, wondering if he should return home, but inwardly knowing that would solve nothing.

Next day, he made a determined effort to forget his problems and contacted his friendly taxi driver. They spent a couple of days doing the tourist trip round Sydney, but Tom could hardly wait for Thursday. Maybe Norrie would have found something for him.

The Hampsons lived in a long, low bungalow, open plan, with a fantastic garden dominated by a swimming pool. Luxuriant bushes sheltered the whole property. Norrie beamed as Tom gazed around.

'It's marvellous, Norrie. A man could forget his worries living in this little lot. A far cry from Shipley.'

Norrie looked at him. 'Sheffield.'

'Oh yes, Sheffield, of course,' Tom smiled outwardly, but inwardly he felt uneasy. He'd been so sure that Norrie had come from Shipley. How could he have forgotten a simple thing like that?

Pat Hampson hadn't changed much either, still bustling about with her usual vitality. She fussed over him at first and Tom enjoyed that, he was very homesick.

'Joyce must miss you terribly,' she said, her eyes full of concern.

'Well, I'm out from under her feet,' he used an expression familiar to them, trying to steer the conversation away from the personal angle.

'I'll never forget the time we took Pat and Joyce to the Rugby League Final,' Norrie said, after they'd swapped family news.

'When was that?' Tom asked, cutting into an enormous steak.

'Your memory's like a sieve, Tom,' Pat said jokingly. 'Surely you haven't forgotten Joyce throwing her shoe at the ref?'

'Oh, yes, yes,' he said hurriedly but not before he'd seen Norrie's worried glance. Norrie knew that he couldn't remember a single thing about the

Final. Even now, with prompting, the whole day was a blank.

A little desperately, Tom turned the talk to building. He was on safer ground there; this was his trade. He knew everything about it.

'I read the report you wrote in the Journal about that new cement,' Norrie said. 'I was very impressed. Have you used it yet?'

'Er, well, I don't know. Those eighteen months, you know . . . ' Tom's voice trailed off.

'You mean you haven't been back at work since the accident?'

'No.'

There was the briefest of pauses, then Norrie began to talk of Australia, the climate and the beauties of Sydney. He spiced all his remarks with some dry Yorkshire humour and Tom began to relax and enjoy himself. He also silently thanked his friend for his thoughtful compassion in taking him out of the spot-light.

Norrie suggested the best places to

visit, the finest sights to see in Sydney and Tom decided he would take his advice.

He made no plans for the next few days, just went where the fancy took him, ate when he felt like it and spent hours on the beach. He sent a bombardment of postcards to Shelley and some more restrained ones to Joyce. Gradually, some of his tension eased and gradually he took on a tan, gained some weight and began to feel more cheerful and hopeful again. Only one small cloud hovered over him. He'd still done nothing about Lisa Donnelly. She had a Sydney address, maybe he should contact her now and get it over with. He decided a telephone call wasn't good enough, that he should make a personal visit.

He took Steve's taxi to the address the following day. It was in a pleasant Sydney suburb, a good place to raise a family, Tom thought.

A middle-aged woman answered Tom's knock on the door and at first he took her for Lisa Donnelly's mother.

'Hello, may I speak to Mrs Donnelly?' he asked her.

The woman shook her head. 'She doesn't stay here now. Went to live with her father after she was widowed.'

His heart sank. 'Do you have her address?'

' 'Fraid not. She's on a cattle station, somewhere in the Outback. Just packed up the kids and went, she was so upset at the time. I sent on some of her furniture to Gillieston, the nearest town. Try the post office there, they might have her address.'

Tom thanked the woman and returned to the car. 'Have you heard of a place called Gillieston?' he asked Steve.

The taxi driver shook his head.

'In the Outback.'

Steve started the car and drove along the road. 'One street, some houses, maybe a school,' he said in his laconic way.

Later that evening, Tom puzzled over

why Lisa Donnelly should have left a lovely house in a good suburb, where there would be a school, friends, sport, everything her children might enjoy as they were growing up, and go to the Outback.

It seemed a crazy decision, and there was only one logical reason for it. She must have been without money. He was appalled. Naturally, everyone back home had taken it for granted that Bill Donnelly had been insured, and since Lisa had not replied to Alan Markham's letter offering help, it was assumed she was in a good financial position.

He sent a cable to Alan Markham that evening, saying he was sure that Mrs Donnelly was in financial straits and asking for ample funds to be made available in Australia for him to draw on.

It wasn't until he'd sent the cable, that he realized he'd already made up his mind to go and see her.

Next day he asked Steve's advice about hiring a car for the journey. The taxi driver was aghast at Tom even contemplating such a trip, but once he saw how determined he was, Steve arranged for a reliable car and even mapped out a route.

Two days later, Tom set off. He felt great. As he drove through the streets of Sydney, he realized how much he'd come to like the place. He felt quite at home. The climate, too, was fantastic and it wasn't even summer yet! He'd almost forgotten what rain was like and that couldn't be bad.

Joyce and Shelley would love it out here, particularly his daughter, who loved all outdoor sports. He began to think seriously of what it would be like to settle in Australia. The prospects kept his mind occupied as he took the route that led over the Great Divide, the range of mountains which separated the east coast from the interior.

He had scoffed a little at Steve's plans for him to stop and rest frequently and he skipped the two first planned halts. Then he found that once in the Outback, the stretches of road between towns seemed longer and longer.

Here the highway was arrow straight, scarcely deviating in any way, with low scrub on either side and the flat plain stretching out forever, broken only by a few rocks and small, sparse trees. The heat was far worse than he had anticipated and the dust was everywhere. He longed just for a cloud or two to give him shade now and then. The sight of a wayside café, with its welcoming verandah giving protection from the sun, could only be compared to finding an oasis in a desert, as far as he was concerned.

He had the sense to make overnight stops, but still he found that he could drive only shorter distances each day. He had a niggling worry that this trip might undo all the good of the long rest in Sydney.

At last he reached Gillieston. It had one long, wide main street, with a central parking area. He turned in and stopped the car, resting his head on the wheel for a moment. He was, as usual, parched and his head throbbed with pain.

By now, he could find a hotel almost by instinct and he slowly made his way across the wide street, noticing there was a bank and a post office, as well as some good shops.

Some men were lounging in chairs on the verandah of the hotel. Tom knew from experience gained at stops in other towns, that he was being sized up as he walked from the car.

'Good day,' he nodded to the group, giving the usual Australian greeting.

Nods and grunts and one 'Good day' answered him.

'Bar's to the left as you go in,' someone said.

He nodded his thanks.

The barman poured his beer, not apparently looking at him.

'First trip to Australia?' he asked.

Tom nodded, amused that the keen eyes had missing nothing.

'Come to work here?'

'No. Just on holiday.' That was the truth, for the moment.

'Picked a funny place to holiday. What about Sydney?'

'Yes, I'm actually staying there. I just came out here to look up some friends.'

'Oh, really?' the barman looked interested.

'Name of Donnelly. I believe they have a cattle station near here.'

'Anybody know a Donnelly who runs a cattle station?' the barman asked, looking beyond Tom.

He became aware that the men from the verandah had drifted into the bar and were now sitting at various tables round the room.

'What's he look like?' someone asked.

Tom turned round. 'I haven't met the family. I only know there is a Mrs Donnelly, with two children and that she lives with her father. I don't know his name.'

'He wants Chet Oliphant,' Someone said from the back of the room. 'His daughter's name is Donnelly. She came from Sydney.'

'That's right,' Tom said.

'You have a way to go yet. Cattle station is at Whangiehill.'

Tom's heart sank. Surely he didn't have to drive even further? Whatever had possessed the girl to come away out here? He'd never seen such unwelcoming landscape in his whole life. All these miles and miles of flat land, yellowing dried grass, stunted trees, never a decent mountain, or lake, to relieve the monotony. He must have been mad to come. He could just as easily have sent a letter or a cheque.

After a few cool drinks and a good meal though, he felt better and once again started on another seemingly endless highway. The directions he'd been given were simple: 'Just keep going until you see the Whangiehill sign'.

He found it. It wasn't much. Fixed to a leafless tree was a long piece of wood with the name 'Whangiehill' branded on it. Underneath it was a mail box nailed to the trunk.

He turned off the highway onto a dirt track and it was another few miles before he saw the fence. A gate, none too sturdy, straddled the track.

Stiffly, Tom opened the barrier, drove through and then closed the gate after him. Some way ahead he could see a building, a now familiar style, long and low, with the usual covered verandah running all the way round.

He approached slowly. There was a small paddock to one side of the house, with a couple of horses grazing on poor grass. A large water tank on stilts and various outbuildings, probably used for storage or garaging completed the layout. 'Cattle station' seemed a bit of an exaggeration in Tom's eye.

A land Rover, as dusty as his own car was parked near the house. He drew in beside it. Nothing happened for a moment or so and he was glad. He needed a quiet moment, to summon up the remnants of his energy to cross to the house.

He'd just got out of the car when a boy of about seven or eight came round from the paddock. His jeans were scuffed and dusty, but his red and white checked shirt was crisp and clean.

As he came nearer, Tom knew at once that this was Bill Donnelly's son. There was the same enquiring air about him, the beginnings of a stride just like Bill's, but as he stopped in front of Tom, it was the directness of the strong blue eyes that tore at his heart. It should have been Bill Donnelly stepping out of this car; he should have been here with his son.

'What are you selling, mister?'

Tom's sadness was somewhat dispelled by amusement at the boy's direct question.

He spread his hands. 'Nothing. I came to see Mrs Donnelly.'

'What about?'

Tom looked at the boy. There was no doubt the child was doing his best to keep out unwelcome callers, but surely he was too young to be entrusted with that?

'I'm from England — ' Tom began.

'Who is it, Neal?' a voice called from the verandah.

Tom looked over towards the house, but the person was still in the shade.

'Somebody to see you, Mum. From England, he says.' The boy still stood between Tom and his mother.

The figure came out of the shade. Lisa Donnelly was taller than he expected. He reckoned she was about thirty, and slim almost to the point of being thin. She wore jeans, of course, a man's checked shirt, the sleeves rolled up to the elbow.

She almost ran down the steps and came forward to where Tom was standing.

He saw now that she had a perfectly proportioned oval face, her skin not yet spoiled by the relentless Australian sun, a strong mouth, neat nose and eyes of a more gentle blue than those of her son. Blonde hair, which could look fantastic, was pulled back from her face and fastened by some kind of clasp.

Her eyebrows were puckered and she didn't look particularly friendly.

'From England you say?'

'Yes,' Tom's voice was a croak his throat was so dry. 'I knew your husband.'

'Go into the house, Neal,' she told the boy. He hesitated, than ran off.

'You knew Bill — do you know what happened to him?' her voice was high.

Tom nodded. They couldn't possibly talk about it out here, in the blazing heat, surely she understood that.

'Do you know the man who killed him?' she asked grimly.

'Killed him?' Tom stared at her. What was she talking about? The sweat was now trickling down his face, saturating his clothes. He swayed a little, took out a handkerchief and began mopping his face.

Suddenly she caught his arm. 'Look, I'm sorry. You're all in. Come into the house,' She led him up the house steps.

He didn't take in much of the interior at first, just made for the first chair he saw and flopped. His head was spinning and he was sure he was going to pass out.

Lisa Donnelly fetched him a drink and towel to dry himself off.

'Sorry, excuse my bad manners,' she said. 'I should have asked you in straight away. I guess it was just . . . England . . . that set me off.'

Tom slung the towel round his neck and lay back in the chair, slowly sipping the drink.

'You know my husband was killed in a car crash there early last year?' her voice was still tight with emotion.

He nodded.

'It was just such a senseless waste of life,' she looked at him. 'Some careless driving on the motorway in the fog and . . . and a life gone. Two kids left. The other man, the driver, he wasn't killed,' she finished bitterly.

Tom looked into his beer. 'This other man . . . he *was* driving?'

She looked at him a little scornfully. 'Stands to reason — Bill would hardly drive in a strange country, the roads are entirely different. You must have found that since coming here.'

He closed his eyes for a moment. He could hardly tell her that he'd been the passenger in that car and that Bill *had* been driving. He'd begged for a chance to drive Tom's Rover. The fog hadn't been around when they'd started out, otherwise he'd never have let Bill take the wheel.

'I had a letter from the company,' she went on. 'They were very sorry and I guess they were. They offered me help and money — ' she stopped and looked closely at him. 'Have you come about that?'

He nodded. It was simpler not to say anything about the accident at the present time. He was too exhausted to cope and Lisa Donnelly was too emotional to handle the truth.

'I don't need their money.'

Tom put down his beer. 'It's

insurance, Mrs Donnelly. I reckon you could do with some. Your husband obviously didn't have any.'

'Yes, he did.'

'Then why did you come out here?'

'What's wrong with here?'

Tom hesitated. 'I went to the address in Sydney that I'd been given. You had a lovely house there, nice area to raise the children. I assumed you'd left as you couldn't afford to live there.'

'I came here to be with my father. Sure, the children could have had all the right things in Sydney, except one. A proper family. My Dad was on his own here and I reckoned it was more important that we all stay together.'

Behind all that aggression there was courage, Tom reckoned, but he said nothing.

'So don't insult me by offering money,' she finished.

'It isn't intended as an insult, Mrs Donnelly,' he said reasonably.

'Nothing will make up for the loss of

Bill,' her voice was low now, without anger.

'I realize that, but it might help.'

Momentarily a shadow crossed her face, then he saw her head come up again, and the return of that proud look.

Instantly he held up his hand. 'Okay, Mrs Donnelly, I won't offend you any more.

He got to his feet. 'I have a job to do, to see that you are all right. I can't force you to take money, but I'll see that the sum the company decided on is transferred to the bank at Gillieston. It will be there if you want it,' he turned away. He couldn't deal with this woman any longer, her pride was an insurmountable obstacle.

He turned to leave.

'Please, don't go yet,' she said unexpectedly. 'Stay and have something to eat with us. I may be bitter about Bill, but I don't expect someone to come all the way from England to see me and go back on an empty stomach.'

She took him into the kitchen where Neal was finishing off some school-work.

'The children have their lessons by radio,' his mother explained.

Tom nodded, remembering how outlying places relied totally on radio communication for so many things.

'I'm finished now, Mum. Can I take him out to the horses?' Neal asked.

Lisa looked at Tom, blushing a little. 'I'm sorry, I haven't even asked your name.'

'Tom. And yes, I'd like to see the horses.'

Outside, he met Kim, Lisa's daughter and a beautiful miniature of her mother. Her face showed promise of beauty and her blonde hair was flowing and unhampered by clips. But Kim, too, had inherited her father's strong blue eyes. Tom remembered Lisa's remark that Bill's death had been such a waste. For a brief moment, he wondered why he hadn't been the one to die in the crash. After all, nobody seemed to need him now.

The children chattered to him, showed him the cattle station. He admitted to himself that they appeared happy and content, and yet . . .

Over the meal, Tom told them about his time in Sydney, keeping the conversation away from the purpose of his visit. Lisa told him of many other interesting places to visit when he returned.

He rose to leave as soon as the meal was over. It was at least a three hour drive back to Gillieston and he was anxious to get away. The situation here was too prickly for a longer visit.

The children went out to the car, while he thanked Lisa Donnelly for her hospitality.

'I think you ought to take the money,' he said bluntly as they walked out to the verandah.

'No, thanks,' her reply was curt.

'I'm not blind, Mrs Donnelly. Even to my inexperienced eye, I can see there are plenty of repairs needed to the house and to the outbuildings.'

He saw the colour rise in her cheeks, but he continued. She needed that money desperately and she must be made to take it.

'The grazing looks pretty poor to me and the children told me that there's been no rain for ages, and the cattle — '

'How dare you question my children!'

'I didn't, they told me, talking just as children do.'

'Let me tell you, my children lack for nothing. Life is good here for all of us and we don't need your charity,' she turned and slammed the porch door behind her.

Tom went down the verandah steps. Never had he met such a wilful and stubborn woman. He stomped towards the car, his head throbbing with anger and frustration.

'Hey, Tom, you got a flat,' Neal told him as he reached the car.

With despair, Tom looked at the flat front tyre.

'Thanks, that's all I need,' he summoned up a rueful smile for Neal.

He got the jack and the spare tyre out of the boot and bent down to unscrew the nuts on the wheel. Already perspiration was running down his face, into his eyes. Already, his mouth was dry and his head was pounding like the breakers on Bondi Beach.

As he gave the jack one turn a searing pain knifed across his chest and his body slumped onto the rough track, sending up a cloud of red dust.

3

This time Tom's memory returned as soon as he recovered from his blackout. He could remember every single thing that had happened since he'd arrived in Australia, right up to the time he'd been about to take his leave of Lisa Donnelly. He was in a bedroom not a hospital ward, so he'd presumably been taken to her house.

He turned over in the bed and thumped the pillow in a mixture of anger and frustration. It would have to happen here! Lisa Donnelly hadn't been at all pleased to see him and he'd further upset her by offering her the firm's money. And now, she'd been forced to give him shelter.

If only he had told her right away that he'd been in the car accident with Bill. Now, the truth would have to come out — he'd have to explain that his blackout was an after effect of the accident. She'd think his carelessness had killed Bill since she didn't know Bill had been driving that fateful day.

He tried to rehearse what he could say to her, how best to broach the subject of her husband's death.

It was better to have it all clear in his mind beforehand.

He lay for a moment, listening and looking around. The outdoor sounds were different here. Different bird calls, strange animal sounds. Of course the Outback was a far cry from his industrial home in England.

He looked around. He was in a small bedroom, square, sparsely furnished. There was a good walnut wardrobe with a matching chest of drawers, a bed and small unmatched bedside table. The walls were painted plain white, without pictures. Blue cotton curtains hung by the window, outside of which the shutters had been closed. The heat was still oppressive.

He heard a small creaking noise and

a bar of light streamed across the room for an instant. Before he could speak, the door closed again, but he heard a voice.

'Hey, Mum. He's awake now.'

A few moments later, the door opened properly and Lisa Donnelly came into the room carrying a tray.

Tom, apprehensive of her reaction, but determined to get it over with, drew himself up in bed.

'Look, I'm sorry about this. There's no need to bring me anything, I can get up.'

'No, you can't,' she answered quickly. 'Doctor says you have to stay in bed.'

'You've called the doctor?' his heart sank. That was it. Even if he'd wanted to, he would never be able to fool a doctor with a little story about a black-out. All the details of the car accident and his resultant coma would have to come out. It was going to be distressing for Lisa Donnelly.

'I spoke to the Flying Doctor on the

radio. It was the least I could do. This is all my fault.'

Tom stared at her.

She flushed. 'I'm the one to say sorry. Not only was I rude and inhospitable to you, I was so wrapped up in my own troubles, I didn't notice you were in a state of exhaustion.'

'Well, not exactly.'

'Heat exhaustion, the doc says,' she smiled. 'He'll fly in to see you if you don't improve, but he says you're all the same out from England. Crazy about our sun, you haven't the sense to go into the shade now and then.'

'Mad dogs and Englishmen,' Tom quoted with a tentative smile.

Lisa laughed. 'Anyway, a week in bed is the cure, doc says. Now drink this lemonade.'

'A week in bed! But I can't.'

'You're on holiday, aren't you?'

'Yes, but I can't impose on you.'

She frowned a little. 'At least let me make amends for my discourtesy.'

Tom was caught in a cleft stick. If he

went, he'd have to tell the truth about his black-out and that would sever any contact between them forever. If he stayed, accepting the Flying Doctor's diagnosis, it would be under false pretences, but it would give him a little more time to coax Lisa into accepting some money from the firm. After all, that was the whole purpose of his visit to her.

He saw that she was watching him anxiously. He nodded, reached over and took the glass of lemonade from the tray. He was committed to a lie, but it was for the sake of her children, and herself.

★ ★ ★

For the next few days, he rested and slept, determined to restore as much energy as possible to his system. But there was always the nagging feeling that he was an unnecessary burden on Lisa Donnelly. She didn't seem to have any help in the house and he heard very little activity from outside, which surely would have been natural on a cattle station.

And where was her father, Chet Oliphant?

On the third morning, he rose when he heard voices, dressed and left the bedroom. He found himself in a narrow hall with several doors leading off. As he hesitated, unsure of where to go, Lisa's son Neal suddenly appeared at the end of the hall.

'Hi, Tom, are you better? You really were crook,' he said.

'I'm okay now, Neal,' Tom told him.

The boy took him into the kitchen where Lisa was busy at the stove. She looked alarmed when she saw Tom.

'Your doctor didn't know that I was going to be so well looked after, I'd make a rapid recovery,' he smiled at her.

'If you're sure you're okay — '

He nodded and sat down at the table beside Kim, Lisa's daughter. She had a great pile of school books beside her.

'School today, Kim?' he asked.

The girl's pretty mouth turned down at the corners. 'Only on the radio,' she muttered.

'I see, you live too far from a school,' Tom commented.

'No, we don't. There's one in Gillieston, only *we're* not allowed to go,' she retorted.

'That's enough, Kim,' Lisa said quietly.

'Well, it isn't fair. We never see any of our friends.' She jumped up from the table as Lisa began to speak again. 'Oh, don't say it again, we can't afford it. We can't afford anything out here,' and she rushed from the kitchen letting the screen door bang behind her.

Lisa poured a glass of orange juice for Tom, but the liquid slopped over the side. He pretended not to notice how her hand was shaking.

'It isn't the money,' she said tightly. 'They went to school in Gillieston when we first came, but now I don't have the time to drive to Gillieston twice a day.'

'Couldn't one of the station hands take them?' he asked.

'Don't have none now,' Neal replied, his mouth full of cereal.

'Any,' Lisa corrected automatically. She turned to Tom. 'We're a bit short handed at the moment. Shortage of labour.'

He said nothing, suspecting that the station wouldn't be short of labour unless it was short of cash. But Lisa Donnelly was full of prickly pride and he'd have to handle this situation very carefully.

The screen door opened again and a man walked in. He was tall and very lithe and although wearing sturdy riding boots and working jeans, he moved across the room with quiet grace.

'Banka, this is Tom,' Lisa said.

A smile creased the traditional broad face of the Aborigine.

'Hello, Tom.'

Tom stood up and they shook hands. 'Glad to meet you, Banka.'

'Banka is dad's right hand man,' Lisa told him.

Banka shrugged, but Tom could see he was pleased at Lisa's statement.

'The fence is down at five mile bend, again, Lisa,' Banka said.

'Oh, no! I wonder if that's the only place.'

'Didn't have time to inspect any further,' he said.

'I'll ride out today and — ' she stopped abruptly and turned back to the stove.

With sudden intuition, Tom realized she was worried about leaving the homestead.

'Can I come with you, or go with Banka?' Neal was on his feet instantly.

'No, you have your lessons,' his mother said.

'Aw heck!'

'I'll be here,' Tom pointed out quietly.

'Well — ' he could see the indecision in her eyes. She was worried about the fencing, but also about leaving the homestead.

'He'll be okay, Mum, I'll look after him,' Neal promised her.

It was almost sundown before Lisa and Banka returned. She looked exhausted.

Kim, her good nature restored, immediately poured some coffee for them and began preparing a meal.

'We covered all the weak areas of the fence and repaired them,' Lisa said, sinking onto a chair.

'I did all my lessons correctly,' Neal told her.

His mother looked sceptical.

'Did you know that Tom is great at arithmatic?'

'And he can speak French,' Kim chipped in.

Lisa looked at Tom and gave a brief nod of thanks.

Later, after the children were in bed and Banka had gone to see to the horses, Tom and Lisa sat on the verandah in the shadowed coolness of the evening.

'I guess I'll be moving on tomorrow,' he said.

'The doc said you were to rest for a week,' Lisa reminded him. 'You'll just pass out again. I know this country; you don't.'

'If I stay, I pay for my keep.'

'That's downright insulting,' she flared.

'I have my pride, too, you know, Lisa.'

He couldn't see her in the dimness, but heard her indrawn breath.

'You helped the kids today with their schoolwork, that's payment enough.'

'Now that's downright insulting to me,' he replied.

'You're just trying to make me take the company's money, some way or another.'

'It seems to me you could use it,' he changed the subject abruptly before she could answer. 'Where is your father, Lisa? Is he ill, in hospital, or something?'

There was a long silence.

'You may as well know,' she said eventually, bitterness in her tone.

'We've had no rain here for ages. The cattle are desperate for water, that's why they keep breaking through fences. Dad's gone off to hire a rig to drill for water. Don't offer me money again, Tom. Cash can't buy rain,' she paused and continued in a quieter tone, 'And don't suggest that I return to Sydney. My place is here with my father. After all, Whangiehill is the children's heritage.'

'I can see that, Lisa, but meanwhile there's just you and Banka to run this whole station while your father is away?'

'That's it. We hire extra labour for the muster, but usually Dad, Banka and I can cope — ' she stopped abruptly.

'So you're a hand short at the moment.'

She didn't reply.

'I'd like to stay until your father returns, as a paying guest.'

'I don't want your charity — ' she began furiously.

'For Pete's sake, woman, don't throw

everything away for pride.' Tom was really angry. 'I know nothing about running a cattle station. I can't help in that respect, but I mean only to stay at the homestead, keep an eye on the children, supervise their school work if you like. All I'll be is just another adult about the place. That's hardly working for my keep.'

After another long silence, Lisa said: 'How long are you on holiday for?'

'As long as I like. I came out to Australia just to look at the prospects.'

'Do you have a family?'

'Yes.'

'Didn't they want to come with you?'

'Not for a long holiday,' he said carefully. 'My wife's got a full-time job and Shelley, my daughter, has just started a college course.'

Lisa seemed to think over what he'd said, but made no comments.

'Chet should be back fairly soon,' she said eventually and got up and went into the house.

Tom sat on for ten minutes or so. It

seemed that Lisa had accepted his offer to stay without actually saying so. She'd be quite a nice girl if it wasn't for her stiff pride, he reflected. He got up and went to his room. He decided to write to Joyce and Shelley, giving the cattle station's address. He might be here another couple of weeks. He had no idea what Lisa's idea of 'fairly soon' would be. Time seemed on a different scale in the Outback.

★　★　★

'But Tom, everyone can ride a horse.' Neal was looking at him with some amazement.

'I can't. I've never sat on a horse's back in my life.'

Neal whooped with laughter and overturned his chair.

'Get up, you idiot,' Kim said. 'Not everybody in the world lives in the Outback.'

'Can I teach you to ride?' Neal asked.

'Why should Tom learn to ride?' Lisa

asked. 'He lives in a town in England where everyone has a car.'

Banka looked up from his breakfast. 'I think it's a good idea.'

Tom caught Banka's eye and knew instinctively that the man not only wanted him to learn to ride, but also to stay at the homestead for the time being. Tom knew he'd been right, things were too much for Lisa and Banka to handle on their own.

After breakfast, Kim and Neal took him out to the small corral where they kept their horses. Lisa had instructed them that Molly, the docile mare, was the best mount for Tom.

Fortunately, Tom had packed a pair of jeans and some casual shirts, so he didn't look too out of place. Banka had given him an old slouch hat which was essential to protect him from the sun.

Mounted on Molly, he had a good view of Whangiehill Cattle Station. There was the long low homestead, another low building which looked like a bunkhouse, stables and a few other outbuildings. Close to the homestead were two huge cylindrical water tanks. Tom guessed the levels must be pretty low in these, as Lisa was making everyone conserve water.

Beyond the buildings the land seemed to stretch forever, broken only to the North by the slight rise that gave Whangiehill its name. The horizon seemed to shimmer under the relentless sun.

An hour later, stiff and sore, as much from laughter at his own ineptness as the discomfort of being in a saddle for the first time, Tom lounged on the rough grass with the children. Kim had fetched lemonade and cookies from the kitchen for them.

'When you can ride properly, we'll go out and help Banka with the fences,' Neal told him.

'I may not be here much longer,' Tom said. 'Anyway, Banka really knows what he's doing, he doesn't need me.'

'Banka likes you being here,' Kim said perceptively.

'Has he always been at Whangiehill?' Tom asked.

'As long as I can remember,' Kim reflected. 'Ever since he came down here from the North. He was born near some place called Banka Banka. That's why we call him that. We can't pronounce his real name, his tribal name that is.'

A few days later, just before sundown, Tom was able to go for a short ride with the children. He hadn't felt so fit for months and he was gradually becoming accustomed to the heat. The vastness of the territory still amazed him, but he was a little reconciled to the harshness. He was beginning to understand some of the many problems associated with running a cattle station and realized that there was a crisis at Whangiehill.

If only Lisa could be persuaded to take some money from the firm, things could be a little easier for her. True enough, he couldn't make rain, but he could make the homestead a little more comfortable, see to repairs, hire some hands, but he knew she wasn't nearly ready to accept anything from him yet. Maybe it was time he moved on, perhaps he could help her more from a distance. He suspected she resented him seeing the hardships they lived with.

As he and the children returned to the homestead, Neal spotted a cloud of dust about a mile away.

'Someone coming to visit us,' he shouted.

'Nobody comes to visit us,' Kim retorted.

'It must be Gramps coming home. Whoopee!'

The children rode a little harder to reach the homestead at the same time as the Landrover.

Tom trotted behind, feeling an irrational sense of disappointment. Chet Oliphant was home and it looked as if he would have to leave. But wasn't that what he wanted?

★ ★ ★

Chet Oliphant was a small, wiry man, with pure white hair and skin hardened and coloured like old leather. He looked to be in his late sixties, much older than Tom had expected. Since he reckoned Lisa's age as around thirty, he had assumed her father would be in his mid-fifties.

He felt even more dismayed at the situation at Whangiehill. An old man, one stockman and a young woman. How could they successfully run a cattle station?

Although it was obvious that he was very tired, Chet was interested in Tom and sorry to hear he'd taken ill.

'A few weeks at Whangiehill and you'll be a new man, Tom. This is the best country in the world for a man.'

Brave words, thought Tom, for a man who looked as if he had taken all the hardships he could cope with. From the soft burr which Chet gave to some words, Tom guessed he was not native to Australia.

'I was a shepherd in Perthshire, back

home in Scotland until I was thirty or so, then I decided to come out here,' Chet told him in reply to his question. 'I worked on sheep and cattle stations for years, but it was hard going.'

'Why did you come to Whangiehill?'

Chet gave Tom a shrewd glance.

'You're wondering why I didn't choose an easier option at my time of life? I'd always had a hankering for my own place and when Whangiehill came on the market at a price I could afford, I just couldn't wait any longer. When I make up my mind to do something, I do it. Just like Lisa here, stubborn as a mule.'

Tom exchanged a brief look with Lisa. He was thinking of her stubborn refusal to take his money, and she knew it. Her look was still defiant.

'Mind you,' Chet went on. 'I had to change my whole way of thinking, adapt to new ideas, but I did it. Lisa thought I was mad.'

'I had just married Bill and moved to Sydney, so I was no help at all.' Lisa said.

'My wife, Lisa's mother, died just two years after we came here,' Chet paused and slowly rolled a cigarette. 'I just wish she'd been with me longer to enjoy this place. She worked so hard for it, too,' he lit his cigarette and looked at Tom through the spiralling smoke. 'That's why I don't want to give it up, throw away all she worked for, too,' he finished quietly.

Tom said nothing. He could respect the old man's determination and loyalty but surely he couldn't expect to succeed over nature? Lack of rain to give water for the cattle wasn't something you could overcome with hard work. No, Chet Oliphant was as stubborn as his daughter and perhaps a little too headstrong to see reason. The only answer to their problem was a cash flow to help in drilling to find water. And that, Tom decided, was something he would see that they took. He could be determined, too.

'The drilling rig, Dad, you did fix that all right?' Lisa asked.

There was a pause, then Chet nodded.

'I've ridden all over the station with Banka this last week,' she told him. 'And we reckon there's at least six possible areas where water might be found.'

This time Chet shook his head. 'I just hired them to sink one hole.'

'*One*? Only one, Dad? But why — '

He gave her an eloquent look and she immediately turned away.

'Oh well, maybe it will be the right one,' she said in a brittle tone so unlike her.

Tom said nothing but he was horrified. It was obvious that one hole was all Chet could pay for. Things were much worse than he thought. One look at Lisa's closed face, however, told him he daren't offer money now. He'd have to see Chet alone, and feel his way, very carefully.

'The crew arrives Saturday, Lisa,' Chet said. 'Will you ask Banka to get the old bunkhouse ready for them?'

★ ★ ★

It was Tom who fixed up the bunkhouse for the crew in the end.

'I reckon Banka is more use to your dad elsewhere on the station,' he said in reply to Lisa's protests next morning. 'And I can manage the bunkhouse.'

'You don't have to work here,' Lisa said brusquely.

'Come on, Lisa,' he said patiently, 'I know that. I just would like to help.'

'I'll go, too, Mum. Tom and I have finished my schoolwork,' Neal chipped in.

Tom raised his hand to stop Lisa's outburst.

'I didn't do his schoolwork, I just explained some things to him.'

'Sure, I don't have problems no more. I mean, any more,' Neal gave his mother a cheeky grin and escaped outside.

Together Tom and the boy first swept out the bunkhouse, then swabbed the floor. While Tom set up the beds, Neal polished the windows. Neal could be a bit unruly and cheeky to Lisa, but underneath he was a good lad. Tom realized he'd grown quite fond of him.

Lisa and Kim brought out some drinks and doughnuts mid-morning. After 'tucker' as Neal called it, they made up the beds while Kim hung fresh cotton curtains at the windows.

Later, they all went for a ride, as Tom had found himself passionately taken with riding. That night he realized he felt better than he had for years. His muscles had toned up, his breathing was fine; no headaches; no fatigue, loads of energy in fact. He was ready now for any job that Norrie Hampson could find for him in Sydney. There was only one more thing he had to accomplish at Whangiehill.

Next day he asked Chet if he could ride out with him to inspect the area where the drilling crew would operate. They set off early before the sun was too high.

To get the old man talking Tom

questioned him about managing the cattle station. He was actually genuinely interested in everything Chet told him, but gradually stage-managed the conversation round to money.

'It must cost you a bit to hire a drilling crew,' he said casually.

'Everything,' he said succinctly.

'Couldn't Lisa help out?'

Chet swung round in the saddle and at once Tom saw from whom Lisa had inherited that prickly pride.

'I came here to give Lisa money from the company,' Tom told him bluntly.

'And she won't take it?' Chet asked.

'No.'

They rode on for a bit in silence then Chet began talking quietly.

'Lisa insisted on joining me here when Bill was killed, and I was very happy to have them. I'd been really lonely since my wife died and it was good to have her and the kids here. But I shouldn't have let them stay.'

Tom said nothing. He realized Chet needed to talk it all out.

'She brought quite a bit of money with her, from the insurance and sale of her house in Sydney, and she wanted to put it all into Whangiehill. She reasoned of course that it would all go to the children in the end, which would be true if there's anything left.

'I wouldn't take all her money. I made her put some in trust for the children. They might want to go away to school; and I wanted her to have some money for her own future. I don't reckon there's much chance she'll find another husband out here. I know she's not looking for one, but someone would have come along in Sydney, and she might have had a secure future again.'

'You could take the company's money, Chet,' Tom said. 'After all, it's for the future of Whangiehill, which means the future of the children.'

'Don't you think my daughter would know if I took it? Besides, I have my pride, too,' Chet replied.

'I am heartily sick of the word 'pride',' Tom exploded. 'This money means you can go on sinking holes until you find water. Do you want your cattle to die, to be sold as a pile of bones?' he finished dramatically.

They rode for a bit in silence.

'I have a favour to ask you,' Chet said. 'I understand you plan to return to Sydney early next week.'

'Yes, that's right. I'm expecting to get a job there.'

'Could I ask you to stay on at Whangiehill for a few weeks?'

'Why?'

'I'd like to be with the drilling crew. They could use some extra help, and I couldn't afford to hire any more men. If I knew you were back at the homestead, helping out, I could leave Lisa with an easy mind.'

Tom thought over all the implications of the request. It was now late November and he'd promised Shelley that he'd be home for Christmas, or he'd fly her and Joyce out to Sydney to spend Christmas with him. A few weeks would probably detain him at

Whangiehill over Christmas and he could hardly ask Lisa to accommodate two more guests, even if they wanted to come to the Outback.

He had really wanted to see Shelley for Christmas. With a pang of guilt, he realized he'd thought very little about Joyce over the past few weeks. And he instinctively knew she wouldn't want to come here for Christmas. He'd better write to them both and put the position to them.

'We really all need you here, Tom,' Chet said persuasively.

Tom mentally shrugged. For the first time in months someone really needed him; not his wife, nor his daughter, nor any of his old friends, but a small, stubborn, proud family he'd only known for about a dozen days.

He suddenly realized that by staying he might after all achieve his purpose in coming to Whangiehill.

'O.K. Chet, I'll stay, on one condition. That if you don't find water at this sink hole, my money pays for future drilling.'

The old man pulled his bush hat down over his eyes.

'Too late for that, Tom. To get the bank to give me money for this operation, I had to sign a contract saying if no water is found this time, I sell up.

'I never told Lisa, but I've had some bad years here and I had to borrow money two years back. There's a mineral company wants to get its hands on the land out at five mile bend and I would have had to sell out to them before if Lisa hadn't put some money into the station.'

'Does she know about the mineral company now?'

'No, no, I just couldn't bring myself to tell her how bad things are.

'But that's the score Tom. We find water, or we're bust. It's all on this one throw. In a few weeks' time, Lisa, the kids and me could be saying good-bye to Whangiehill.'

4

'I don't want him to stay!' Lisa said, glaring at her father.

'But I do! He's my guest,' Chet replied, staring defiantly back at his daughter.

Tom sat at the supper table in a state of acute embarrassment. Immediately after their return from inspecting the drilling site Chet had told Lisa that Tom was staying on for a while to help out. Now she was reacting with the fiery temperament which she'd obviously inherited from her father.

'I want Tom to stay,' Neal piped up.

Lisa quelled him with a glare.

'And I'd like him to stay.'

Tom was surprised, and very touched, when he heard Kim speak up bravely, despite her mother's obvious anger. Tom gave the girl a brief smile. He knew that Neal regarded him as a friend, but he hadn't realized that Kim liked him, too.

Lisa swung round to look at Tom, her face pink with anger and her eyes flashing.

'This is nothing personal against you, Tom, please understand that,' she said quickly. 'It's just what you stand for.'

'Chet won't take my money either, if that's what's bothering you,' he answered her with more coldness than he really felt. He liked the girl, but she was positively obsessed with not accepting help of any kind.

'You actually offered money to him?' she demanded brusquely.

'I had a job to do,' he told her. 'I haven't succeeded, so let's forget it. Chet just asked me to stay on for a couple of weeks. I'm interested in Whangiehill, so I accepted.'

For a moment Lisa stood staring at Tom, a large casserole momentarily forgotten in her hands.

'I like it here,' he finished simply.

Slowly she lowered the dish onto the table and a hint of remorse passed across her face, but she said nothing more and quickly dished up the plates of stew.

Later, after the children had gone to bed and Chet was down at the corral with Banka, Tom broached the subject again.

'Let's sit on the verandah for a bit, Lisa,' he said to her. 'I think we ought to get one or two things straightened out. The air is cooler out there.'

He was relieved to see the quick flash of laughter in her eyes at his last remark. All was not lost when she still had a grip on her sense of humour.

They stretched out on loungers on the verandah but were silent for a little while. Tom had to get his thoughts in order in his head.

'There are no strings attached to my staying on,' he began. It was true. He would have given Chet the money meant for Lisa, but it would be no use to him as he didn't have time left to use it. But since Lisa didn't know the full facts of the situation he certainly wasn't going to tell her. That was Chet's worry.

'In a way, I'm a man with nowhere to go at the moment. A friend in Sydney is keeping an eye out for a job for me but it will be a few weeks before something comes up, I reckon. Until then my time is my own.'

'Aren't you going back to England then?' she asked.

'I'm not sure,' he said.

He didn't want to tell her about the strained situation between his wife and himself. He still wasn't sure how he felt about it himself.

'I like Australia. If I can find the right opportunity — ' he left it like that.

'And your wife and daughter will come out and join you?'

He didn't know the answer to that question.

'Well, if my glowing reports of your beautiful country haven't convinced them by now, nothing will,' he said evasively.

'You like . . . all this,' Lisa waved her hand at the endless vista of scrub. 'I mean, how does it compare with your home?'

'Chalk and cheese,' he said. 'At home I'm surrounded by trees, hills and rivers. I live in a neo-Georgian house with French windows leading on to a beautiful lawn. All that will be Shelley's one day. But today, riding back to Whangiehill with your father, I somehow felt it just didn't compare with what you have here, the heritage that will be your children's. Anyone with money can buy my house, put it down in attractive parkland.'

Tom got up and went to lean on the verandah rail. 'But this — this has to be fought for, a constant battle against nature,' he turned to Lisa. 'It's worth fighting for. Even if it's only for a few short weeks, I'm enjoying being part of it.'

Lisa walked over to stand beside him.

'I've misjudged you, Tom,' she held out her hand. 'I'm sorry.'

Tom took her hand. He knew how much it must have cost someone with Lisa's strong personality to say sorry. 'I'm not looking for apologies, they aren't called for. I'm just glad to know that we're on the same side.'

'Let's get some beer and drink to that,' she smiled at him.

They sat for some time swapping stories of childhood, and Tom tried to convey to her the rugged beauties of the Yorkshire Dales. He realized she was hungry for details of life on the other side of the world.

'I think maybe you have to see it, to believe it,' he finished.

'Bill was going to bring home a suitcase full of photographs, but he never even managed that.'

'Can you accept his death now, Lisa?' he asked gently.

'I can live with it, but I will never accept his killing. Never will I forgive the man driving that day.'

Tom decided that was one subject he would never again raise with Lisa.

Nothing would make her accept that Bill had been driving that day.

Two days later the drilling crew arrived and Chet went off with them to help out with the work. Tom knew nothing about drilling, so he reckoned he would be no use to them, and would only get in the way.

Besides, there was plenty of work on the homestead. He attacked the peeling paintwork first, scraping off the remnants of the old, then applying new. He worked hard, trying to keep out of the way of the sun, racing it round the homestead. Next, he mended all the fences he could find around the buildings and painted those too.

He'd been tactful enough not to ask Lisa to buy some new paint, and he just used up what he could find. The effect around the homestead was, to say the least, rainbow-hued.

'I never thought I'd like pink window frames with blue doors, but I guess it grows on you,' Lisa laughed.

'Wait till you see the verandah when

I've finished. Did I tell you I only have orange paint left?'

'In future, I'll only go out there in the dark,' she retorted.

Tom was glad of the hard work. The weekly mail had brought him letters from home. Shelley's letter, as usual, was full of the things she was doing at college. There was no mention of him, beyond enquiries after his health and admonitions to behave himself. It seemed as if Shelley was quite used to living without him. Of course, eighteen months out of their lives had seen to that, never mind coming to Australia.

He could glean nothing from Joyce's letter. It, too, was full of concern for his health, but there was no query as to when he was returning home, or how he felt about their marital situation. She filled the pages with news about the building trade and little else. There wasn't even anything to read between the lines. In fact; he had the strong feeling that Joyce had really nothing to say to him. Was that why he was

107

involving himself at Whangiehill, to give him something to care about?

★ ★ ★

It had somehow become a habit for Lisa and himself to sit together on the verandah in the evenings. Sometimes Chet joined them, but usually he was too bushed after working all day at the drilling rig.

'Tom, what do you think I should do about Kim and Neal concerning schooling?' Lisa asked one evening.

He considered the question for a long time.

'I think Kim might benefit from the company of other girls, but then again, she could be awfully homesick away from Whangiehill and you'd miss her dreadfully.'

'That isn't the point.'

'No, I know you wouldn't be selfish enough to keep her here. I'd delay a decision for a bit, though. She's only twelve. How about giving her another year, maybe two?'

He couldn't tell her that there was a strong possibility the whole family could be back in Sydney in a few weeks, if no water was found.

'And Neal?'

'He's okay at the moment. He loves the life here,' he told her.

'Too much, maybe. He doesn't attend to his schoolwork.'

'Does any boy at his age?'

She laughed. 'I guess not. Thanks anyway, I think you've helped me get the situation in perspective. Oh, drat,' A large folder fell onto the floor.

'What on earth is that anyway?' he asked.

'The accounts book. I have a go most nights, but I guess Neal inherits his non-mathematical brain from me.'

'Pass it over. I used to do the accounts for my firm when I was on the bottom rung of the ladder.'

'No, Tom, you do enough here.'

'Come on, Lisa. I'm not going to put any money into Whangiehill, but let me see if I can save you some.'

He was appalled when he studied the accounts. Chet obviously didn't have a business head either. A whole lot of money had been going down the drain regularly at Whangiehill.

Tom worked late into that night trying to see if any last ditch efforts could be made to restore some money to the cattle station by pruning some expenses. Although engrossed in his task, he was the first to hear the radio crackling. But he could make out nothing of the signal so he went to waken Lisa.

Expertly she flicked the switches and then Tom heard the message loud and clear. A neighbouring station owner was reporting that Chet's herd had broken through a fence and was now on his property. His voice was terse and the command short: 'Get them rounded up and back on your own station.'

'You and Banka can't cope with this, can you?' Tom asked as Lisa hurried from the room.

'No. I'll have to waken the children,' she said in a tight voice.

'I'm coming too,' he called.

She didn't protest and that, more than anything, told Tom how serious the situation was. Lisa would never let him take part in anything like this if she could possibly help it.

Fifteen minutes later, with Banka leading the way, they set off for five-mile bend, where the cattle had once again broken through. Chet, still out with the drillers, knew nothing of it.

Lisa had instructed everyone to dress warmly but even then Tom was surprised at how cold it was. They rode hard, under the starlit sky, on and on, over the endless scrub, broken only now and then by a eucalyptus tree. They heard a few night creatures, but saw none. It was the first time that Tom had been so far from the Station homestead.

The stretch of fence at five-mile bend had been flattened by the cattle. It would take some time to repair, but

Tom knew it would have to be done as soon as they drove the cattle back to Chet's land.

After about another three miles of dry dusty plain, Tom could see shapes outlined in the pale moonlight. As they drew nearer, it was easy to distinguish men and horses, then some cattle. Tom was horrified when he saw the beasts moving restlessly within the circle of riders; the cattle looked thin and undernourished.

A man rode out to meet them.

'This is Matt Wylie, owner of Coombs Bar station,' Lisa introduced Tom to the middle-aged man sitting erect in his saddle.

'I'm sorry, Matt,' she said stiffly.

He shrugged. 'Lucky for Chet it is only part of his herd. You might have had a stampede on your hands; the beasts are getting desperate for good grazing.'

'We still have grazing,' she said sharply.

Even in the moonlight, Tom could

see the scepticism in Matt Wylie's face.

'I hear tell that Chet is drilling a well. Has he hit water yet?'

'No.'

'Time's running out, Lisa. He'll have to sell those cattle soon before they get any leaner.'

'We'll reach water any day now.'

Matt nodded. 'Hope so. Anyway, my hands will help with the fencing.'

Tom saw Lisa's hands tighten on her reins. He knew the signs, she was going to refuse the offer.

'We'd appreciate that, Mr Wylie,' he said quickly. 'Lisa has to take the children back, so there's only Banka and me.'

She whirled in her saddle to glare at Tom, but before she could speak he leaned over and put his hand on her shoulder.

'I know you are capable of helping us fix it, but I really think the children ought to go back to bed.'

With some reluctance, she agreed. Tom watched the little family ride off;

Lisa Donnelly was a game girl, he'd say that for her. And yet her husband, Bill Donnelly, had given everyone in England the impression that she was a frail, helpless type. Perhaps only now in adversity her real personality was coming through.

★ ★ ★

It was early dawn before Tom and Banka returned to Whangiehill and it wasn't until he slipped down from the saddle, sore and stiff, that Tom realized he had lasted through the long night of hard riding and strenuous work, without once feeling exhaustion or nausea. He'd stood up to everything. Did this mean he was fully returned to health? As he slipped off his warm jacket, he reflected how tough his body was now, all muscle and no fat. He even looked younger. The sun had bleached his hair, tanned his skin. I'd give Alan Markham a run for his money any day, he thought. But no, that wasn't true. He wasn't interested in competing with his former business partner any more. Not only did he look different, he *was* different, *inside*. But he was too tired to analyse that right now.

Lisa had food and hot coffee waiting for them. Banka ate and drank silently but Tom couldn't hold his tongue.

'We have to thrash this out, Lisa. I've been ignorant about the state of this cattle station until now. But last night Banka and I drove the cattle back to join the herd. Even to my eye, the grazing is almost non-existent. Acres of grass, just brown and burned up. Okay, there is one area still irrigated enough to give some decent grazing, but no longer sufficient for the whole herd.'

She didn't reply.

'It may last until Chet finds a new well, but the cattle are going to keep straying over to Matt Wylie's property. You need extra hands to patrol that fence. Matt isn't going to be so co-operative next time.'

Still she kept silent.

'Two extra hands, just for the few weeks it takes to find water,' he persisted.

'And you'll pay, I suppose? The answer is no, Tom. The answer will always be no, can't you get that into your head? I'm beginning to think there's more to this money. Is it really from the man who was with Bill that day, is it his conscience money?'

'No,' Tom shouted, but she'd already slammed out of the kitchen.

They didn't see much of each other for the rest of the day, as everyone was catching up on lost sleep.

That night Chet and the drilling crew returned to the bunkhouse. They needed some time off and a rest. Tom didn't go out on the verandah after supper, but made straight for the bunkhouse. He'd met the crew on their arrival, but had so far not discussed the problem with them.

Mike Yarrow, in charge of the crew, saw Tom coming over.

'Hi, heard you went for a midnight ride,' he joked.

'A ride that should never have happened,' Tom said and sat down on the bunkhouse steps beside him.

'Too true,' Mike flicked a cigarette end into the dust. There was something very straightforward about the driller. Around twenty-five years of age, not too tall, but well-muscled, he was dressed in the usual gear of checked shirt and denims. His face, already weather-beaten, was open and honest.

'How is it going?' Tom asked him.

Mike rubbed a hand against a day's beard. 'I don't like it. We're still drilling through rock. If there's water down there, I reckon we ought to have found it by now.'

'Could Chet be wrong about that site?'

Mike shrugged. 'Not necessarily. This is the area of the Great Artesian Basin with a network of underground streams. And Chet says there was a spring at this site many years ago. I reckon we could find water anywhere, but time is our enemy. Obviously we want to drill where the water is as near the surface as possible. We could reach water quicker by moving the rig.'

'Won't Chet agree to that?'

'No. I reckon he's banking on us finding water any day now and if so, he'll be able to pay us off quickly.'

'To move the rig would take more money and time?'

'More money, but less time if we find water quickly. I heard you were willing to stake out some more drilling, anything to help save the station, but they won't accept.'

Tom looked at him in surprise.

Mike grinned. 'We invented the bush telegraph, remember?' His face became serious again. 'I know this mineral company that's trying to buy Chet's land. They're pretty ruthless. They won't give Chet a day longer and they won't cry over his troubles.'

'Keep that quiet, Mike. Lisa doesn't know about it yet.'

'I reckon she does now. Chet decided to tell her tonight.'

'Oh, no!'

The news would shatter Lisa. But would it change her mind about accepting some money?

'Say listen, have you talked to Banka about locating a well?' Mike asked.

'No, why?'

'Well, as you know the Aborigines are originally hunters, and they have fantastic knowledge of where to find food and water even in the most desolate landscapes. This knowledge is passed down the tribes over the years. Some places are sacred to various tribes and he might be frightened to disturb spirits. That's against the tribal law. He wouldn't be allowed to search for water, but *we* would as we aren't members of the tribe.'

'I'll talk to him rightaway,' Tom said. 'If he comes up with anything we might persuade Chet to change the location of the drilling.'

'You can only try.' Mike sounded sceptical.

Banka was nowhere to be found. Tom

knew he went off some nights on his own, he'd no idea where, and had never pried. If only he hadn't gone off tonight. Tom was now of the opinion that practically every minute counted in finding a well.

He didn't see Lisa at first on the verandah. She was tucked away in the far corner, deep in the shadows. When he realised she was there, he knew Chet had spoken to her about the mineral company. There was a tenseness and stillness about her body, as if she was holding herself in check. All the pain and worry was locked up inside her and that wasn't good.

He pulled a chair up beside her lounger.

'Lisa, you must make Chet see reason,' he said, a little harshly.

'Go away, Tom.'

He ignored her. 'I've been talking with Mike. He isn't too optimistic about the present site. He'd like to try elsewhere and he also suggested that Banka might know of some ancient water holes.'

'Banka has been outlawed from his tribe. I don't know why. I never asked, but he'll tell us nothing. Tribal law,' her voice was flat, uninterested. 'Another point, Chet's been here for years. Mike came last week.'

'For crying out loud, Lisa! You are an intelligent woman. Chet's been wrong about a lot of things.'

'Such as?' she blazed.

'Probably buying this place at his age in the first place,' he said brutally. 'And frankly he's lost a great deal of money by bad management. It's all there in the accounts.'

'Mr Know-All, our saviour, come to stitch Whangiehill station together again, show the inept amateurs how it really should be done. A neo-Georgian house, a fancy car, a big company and you think you can run the world.'

Tom was appalled. Did she think that of him? Then he realized she was crying. Lisa Donnelly was *crying*.

'Hey, hey, come on now, Lisa,' awkwardly he went over to her and patted her shoulder, just as he might have done with a tearful Shelley, or Kim.

'Tom, I'm sorry, that was stupid and nasty of me,' she sobbed. 'It's just that I see everything slipping away from me. There will be nothing for the children. Nothing. What have I done to them by bringing them out here?'

She jumped up and went over to the verandah rail and stared out at the vast acres of Whangiehill. Tom stood behind her for a moment, then slowly put an arm round her shoulders.

'I think you did the right thing in bringing them here,' he told her.

She turned to him, with a look of surprise in her eyes.

'You do?'

He nodded. 'You could have brought them up in Sydney with everything kids want from life, but they might not have achieved anything except the empty possessions I gained in England. They mean nothing. Kim and Neal are beginning to learn what life is really about, the struggle, the battle, but most of all, caring. That is life, Lisa.'

Slowly she smiled through her tears. 'Yes, it is. And it's part of the problem, too. I care about Chet and this is killing him.'

'He doesn't need to lose Whangiehill, but there isn't much time.'

'The mineral company are breathing down our necks. Three weeks to find water,' she sighed.

'Moving the rig might shorten the odds. It would be money well spent, in my opinion.'

Tom was pushing home the point that to move the rig around meant money and that meant accepting the company's offer. He knew that Lisa was following his line of argument precisely.

'This money isn't mine to give, Lisa. If you won't take it, then I'm prepared to sell my house in England to set up capital for you. I know I'll get my return. There is water somewhere in Chet's land. This station could be great again.'

She gave him a long look. He could see the mixture of pride and stubbornness, but there was also a grudging admiration and, he suspected, thankfulness in her gaze.

'I've miscalled you, been unforgivably rude to you, insulted you since you came here, Tom, but I'm mightly glad you've been here these last few weeks.'

'You've given me a rough ride,' he grinned at her.

She looked him full in the face. 'I'll speak to Chet about taking the company's money, Tom.'

There was no wild sense of achievement, no satisfaction that he'd got his way at last. Tom knew how much the decision had cost Lisa. He only prayed that there was still time for the money to do any good.

★ ★ ★

She was distraught at breakfast next morning.

'I didn't get a chance to speak to dad.

124

He must have ridden out before sun-up,' she told Tom.

'We have to act on our own then. I'll drive into Gillieston today and have the money transferred to your account.'

She hesitated. 'No, Tom. I have to ask him first. I owe him that.'

'Lisa, we can't wait. Every day wasted gives us less time to operate elsewhere. Look, I'll ride out to the rig and speak to him, O.K.?'

'You can try,' she said.

As Tom saddled up his horse, he knew he had another battle on his hands. It had been difficult enough to get Lisa to accept the money, but to make Chet accept, on condition that Mike drilled elsewhere, was going to be very difficult. The old man would have to swallow his pride, twice. That wasn't easy for a man of Chet's age and disposition.

Tom rode mile after mile along the dusty track made by the wheels of Mike's truck. Finally, through the haze of heat, he saw the outline of the derrick structure of the drilling rig. Closer to the site, he could hear the hum of the generator which powered the drill now steadily boring into the rock.

Mike and Chet, almost unrecognizable in protective headgear, were standing some way from the site and the noisy vibrations of the drill, studying rock samples from the bore.

'How is it going?' Tom asked.

'Rock still,' Chet said briefly. 'But I know the sedimentary basin is down there, just a little deeper. Keep going, Mike.' He turned away from the younger man.

'What brings you here, Tom?'

Tom hitched the horse to a fencing post and he and Chet went to sit in the shade of the truck. Over a billy of tea, Tom told him about Lisa's decision to accept the money.

'If Lisa wants to take the money, that's okay by me,' he said finally.

'It's for Whangiehill, Chet, and the sake of the cattle. They need some fresh grazing, and fast. Mike thinks — ' he stopped when he saw Chet's eyebrows meet over his eyes. 'Look, I know nothing about drilling for water — '

'Too true,' Chet was succinct.

'But Mike's had a lot of experience. How about drilling on another site?'

'Is that a condition of accepting the money?' the old man squinted at Tom.

Tom was very tempted to demand that it was.

'Because if it is, Lisa can keep the damned lot,' Chet said. 'This is my place,' he waved his hand around the expanse surrounding them. 'I've been a long time in this country. My eyes, my ears, even my finger tips tell me things. I just know there's an underground stream down there,' he pointed to where the drill was operating.

Tom realized that nothing was going to move the man.

'Would you agree to putting a time limit on this operation here, Chet? Say a few days, then if the hole is dry, you'll move to another location?'

'Sure, but I say when we stop drilling here.'

Tom and Mike had to be satisfied with that. Behind Chet's back, Mike's shrug was expressive and Tom flashed him a sympathetic smile. It was all they could do.

Tom began the long ride back to Whangiehill. He hadn't achieved everything, but at least it was something. Something that might save Whangiehill for Lisa and the children. Chet had saved his pride by letting Lisa accept the money, and by forcing a few more days drilling at his chosen location.

Still, Tom felt a certain satisfaction in that he'd inched nearer a possible salvation for the cattle station. It was with a lighter heart that he rode into the corral, attended to his horse and then walked into the homestead.

As he did so, he heard the crackling of the radio. His first thought was that the cattle had broken through the fences again, and he ran into the room where Lisa was sitting listening.

Slowly she turned to look at him. Her face was tight with bitterness.

'Yes, Mrs Price, your husband has just walked in,' she said into the microphone. 'I'll give him your message. I'm sorry we can't tie up the radio any longer. Goodbye.'

Tom said nothing. His stomach was knotted with anxiety.

Although she'd switched off the radio, Lisa's knuckles still showed white where she gripped the head-set.

'That was your wife, Joyce. She phoned Gillieston and they relayed the phone call on the radio to me.'

'And the message?' he asked urgently.

'Your daughter Shelley wants to see you. She's flying out of Heathrow in four hours' time.'

'*What?*' It was the last thing he expected.

'There's nothing wrong, according to your wife. The college term has finished and she just wanted to come to Australia.'

'But how will she get to Whangiehill?

I think I'll maybe have to go to Sydney to meet her,' he looked apologetically at Lisa.

'I think you will,' Lisa's voice was very cool. 'I'll phone and arrange for the Flying Doctor service to pick you up, if possible.'

'Hey, that's very good of you; I'll reach Sydney very quickly then.'

'I couldn't agree more. And Whangiehill will be rid of you very quickly . . . '

Tom stared at her. 'What did you say?'

'You heard. I can't wait to see the back of you. I never want to see you again. Ever!'

'What's gone wrong, Lisa?' he asked harshly.

'I've just found out the truth about you from your wife. 'How is Tom?' she asked. 'Any more blackouts?' Then she told me all about your coma, how you were still recovering from it. A coma which you suffered after a car crash, the very one that killed my husband, Bill,'

Lisa stood up. She was shaking from head to toe.

'All this fine talk of money from the company. Money you'd give me, you'd sell your house, your car to help. I believed it; I trusted you, and all the time it was guilt money. Conscience money. You were trying to atone for the crash that killed Bill. You don't buy your way out of something like that. We wouldn't touch that money if we were starving in the street!

'Get out. Get away from Whangiehill and stay away!'

She turned and ran from the room.

5

Tom wasted no time in packing his suitcase. He knew it was pointless to try to reason with Lisa. He should have been absolutely honest with her from the very beginning. To say now, that he'd concealed the fact he'd been with Bill when the car crashed in order to persuade her to accept compensation money from the company, sounded weak and contrived.

When he was ready to leave, he went to find her. She was in the kitchen, scrubbing every available surface.

'I'm leaving now by car. I'd rather not wait for the plane.'

She nodded, then said stiffly, 'You won't be in time to meet your daughter in Sydney if you go by road.'

'I realize that. I'll cable from Gillieston, arrange hotel accommodation for her. She'll be safe there until I arrive.'

Lisa continued with her scrubbing.

'Please say goodbye to Kim and Neal for me, and Chet, too.' He was glad the rest of the family weren't around at the moment. He'd been a friend to all, and would have hated to see the betrayal in their eyes.

'I admit I wasn't entirely straight with you, Lisa, about some things — '

Her head shot up at his words and he saw the pain in her eyes.

'But I was *not* driving that car.'

He turned and walked out of the homestead.

The car started immediately and he shot away from Whangiehill without one backward glance. Even when he had to get out of the car to close the gate in the perimeter fence of the property, he completed the task with total detachment. He projected his mind only on to his next problem: Shelley's arrival in Sydney.

The drive to the town of Gillieston didn't take long. He drove fast, still refusing to think about Lisa. At the Post

Office, he cabled a message to await Shelley's arrival at Sydney airport and then booked two rooms in the hotel he'd first stayed in on his arrival in Australia.

He was completely shaken by his daughter's sudden flight to Australia. He'd thought she was so happy at college in England. Perhaps he'd been too wrapped up in the problems at Whangiehill to read between the lines of her letters. Christmas was only two weeks away and maybe she wanted to be with him then, since they'd missed last Christmas together when he was in the coma.

The journey between the Outback and Sydney, which had seemed so endless, so exhausting, a few weeks ago, now passed quickly with no problems and in half the time. He arrived at the Sydney hotel just in time for dinner. The waiter pointed out his table and he saw Shelley sitting there, staring into an orange juice and looking a little lost.

He walked eagerly to the table and

she must have sensed his approach as she lifted her head. She stood up immediately, a look of total surprise on her face.

'Hello, my love.' He caught her arms and gently kissed her.

'Dad, you look . . . terrific.' She was smiling yet her eyes were filled with tears.

Tom guessed she was on the edge of breaking down completely and knew she'd hate that to happen in the crowded dining room.

'I can't tell whether you think that's good or bad,' he teased, gently easing her back into her chair and then sitting opposite her to shield her from the eyes of the other diners.

'I mean you look so well, so good-looking, different somehow.' She attempted a smile, then dropped her eyes and searched for a handkerchief.

He stretched his hand across the table and caught her free one, just quietly holding it for the next few minutes, until she got over the peak of her emotions. He ordered fruit juice for himself, steaks for each of them and a bottle of wine. Soon, with the excellent recuperative powers of youth, Shelley was tucking into her steak.

'I'm sorry Dad, if I dragged you away from your new job,' she said. 'I could have travelled out to Whangiehill myself. I'm dying to see the place, you've told me so much in your letters.'

'The job out there is finished,' he said, not elaborating. 'I'm not going back. Come on, have some more wine.' He filled her barely touched glass, to distract her from questions about Whangiehill.

He was rather anxious to find out just why she'd flown out to Sydney on her own, but knew she'd have to tell him in her own time.

'We'll have Christmas here in Sydney,' he laughed. 'I'm becoming quite used to having turkey and trimmings in the sun,' referring to the Christmas dinner Shelley had cooked when he'd returned from hospital.

She still said nothing and he knew he'd have to ask the question he'd been dreading.

'Why didn't you wait and fly out with your mother?'

'I don't think she's coming.'

'I see.'

'You don't look surprised, Dad.'

'No. I'm . . . I'm not.'

'I want to know why. I am your daughter, I think I have the right to — ' Her voice was rising again, tight with anxiety.

'Finish your coffee, love, and we'll go upstairs.'

No sooner had they entered his bedroom, than Shelley turned to face him.

'Did you come to Australia because you were leaving mother?'

Tom settled himself in an armchair, but Shelley, still tense, perched on the end of his bed.

'I have not left your mother,' he said quietly.

'Are you ever going back?'

'Yes, of course, if she wants me to. I'd rather like it if she came out here though,' he heard himself saying those words; he hadn't realized he'd grown so fond of the country.

Shelley was staring at him, her hands bunched in her lap.

'And if she doesn't want to come?'

'Then I'll have to accept that, Shelley.'

'It's all Alan's fault, isn't it? He's broken up our family,' she burst out.

Tom rose and went over to the bed. He put his arm round his daughter and gave her a gentle hug. Shelley hadn't been blind to the situation after all.

'No, my pet, it isn't all Alan's fault.'

He led her over to a long seat under the window.

'Your mother and Alan didn't set out to fall in love. He was the help and support your mother desperately needed when I was unconscious. Eighteen months is a long time to be without a husband, and Alan gave his help and his time probably out of

138

loyalty to me, that has to be admitted. As time went by, they both probably came to admire qualities in each other, qualities which perhaps only surface in times of stress,' he paused and thought involuntarily of Lisa Donnelly. He'd come to admire her resilience and loyalty to her family during their crisis.

'Alan and your mother probably loved each other long before they realized it. I can't blame either of them, Shelley. Nobody can. After all, they were thrown together in *our* interests.'

'Yes, I know,' she mumbled. 'He was kind to me, too, and I still like him.' She looked apologetically at Tom.

'So do I,' he admitted.

'If you weren't leaving mum, why did you come here?' she asked now.

'I needed time to think, as did your mother, to see if we could save our marriage. Your mother offered to resign her job and never see Alan again, you know, but that wasn't the answer.'

'You did mean to return to England some time?'

'Of course! This was only intended as a holiday.'

'Was?'

Tom realized again he'd spoken subconscious thoughts. He did like Australia. He could make a life here if necessary, but Shelley came first.

'I've been working,' he avoided the direct implication of Shelley's question.

'But you'd like to settle here,' she said shrewdly.

'Perhaps.'

'Will . . . will you and mother divorce?'

'If she wants to marry Alan, I wouldn't stand in her way.'

It was a formal statement, but Tom had an instinct that it signalled an end to his marriage. There was no doubt that he and Joyce had really drifted apart. She wasn't willing to join him here and he wasn't willing to travel home to be with her. It was a very sad way to end a twenty-year marriage.

He saw that Shelley was quietly sobbing now. If only this could have happened without her suffering, but life didn't come ready-cushioned, not for him, not even for his beloved daughter for whom he would have done anything possible. He could no longer give her the stability and security of a united family.

There was nothing else he could say to Shelley and after a few moments she went to her own room.

Tom booked a call to Joyce to tell her of Shelley's safe arrival. When it came through, they talked generally for a few moments, then he spoke bluntly.

'I've told Shelley all about us, although I think she'd guessed.'

'How did she take it?' Joyce asked.

'She's very upset, gone to bed now,' he paused. 'Joyce, have you had time enough to think things over?'

There was a long silence at the other end of the line and that told him everything. Had she really wanted their marriage to revive she would have said so immediately. Guilt, and reluctance to hurt him, were silencing her.

'I've had time,' he said. 'I think it's best that we should part.'

'Oh, Tom,' he heard her sob, but he knew her guilt was compounded with relief.

'No hard feelings, O.K. girl?' he used an affectionate name from their early years together. He rang off then. He knew it was up to him to end the call and not prolong the distress for either of them. They'd had such a good marriage until his accident.

★ ★ ★

He sat in the darkened room for a long time, sunk in depression. It was some time later when he heard a timid knock at his door. Shelley stood there, waif-like in her dressing gown. She was barely over the threshold before the words came tumbling out.

'You're not going to send me back, are you, Dad?'

'Send you *back*?'

'I mean if you are going to stay here

forever. I came out to Australia because I want to be with you.'

'Are you saying you'd stay here if I wanted to?' he asked.

She nodded.

'What about your mother?'

'I still love mum, always will and I'd go and see her often, but . . . but she'll have Alan, she won't really need me; you only have me.'

'What about your college course?'

'I failed my exams, maybe I could start afresh here?'

Tom thought back to the day he'd left England. He had been so sure that Shelley would be happy at college, that she was ready to strike out on her own. Had he been wrong? Had she been unhappy at college because she thought he'd left her forever? Only worry or unhappiness could have caused her to fail exams; she was a clever girl.

He put his hands gently on her shoulders.

'Shall we try to make a life here in Australia, together?'

She nodded, smiling, tears coursing down her face. He held her tightly in his arms. He felt as if he'd been given a second chance in life. He hadn't lost his daughter, she still loved and needed him. Now he had somewhere to go; a purpose to his life. They'd make a home together in this new country.

★　★　★

Tom slept little that night; he did a lot of hard thinking. He didn't think of the past though, memories of the life he had shared with Joyce would come back to him, unbidden, throughout the years ahead, he knew that. Nor did he think of the last few weeks which he'd spent with the family at Whangiehill. That was an episode which he'd completely messed up. There seemed no way he could make retribution to Lisa now.

Instead, he projected his thoughts forward, planning what would be best for Shelley. The initial tears were over, a decision had been made, but Tom knew the next few weeks would be difficult for her. She'd be very homesick.

His first thought was to take her on a luxurious holiday, but then he realized that a succession of impersonal hotels might underline the rootlessness of their new life style.

What they needed was somewhere secure. He could take an apartment here in Sydney for a few weeks anyway, until he was settled in a job. He knew he was completely fit now and looked it. He was prepared to turn his hand to anything. He was a hard worker and the Australians would accept him for that.

Next morning he and Shelley set off apartment-hunting. He decided to give her as much choice as possible, knowing that it would keep her mind off Joyce and home. Two days later, she had found her ideal. It was on the second floor of an elegant block with a wonderful view over Sydney. It had two bedrooms, a large living room, a kitchen streamlined enough to please Shelley and a cool-looking bathroom.

The rooms weren't particularly well decorated but the furniture was solid and comfortable.

'Dad, this is magnificent,' Shelley danced around the living room then opened the doors onto the balcony. 'Are you sure we can afford it?'

'For the time being,' he temporized. 'You do realize that your role as housewife begins this minute?' he teased.

She looked mystified.

'Here, take this money, go and find some food. I'll go back to the hotel and collect our luggage.'

It took them only a few days to settle into the flat and he soon found that his daughter was a very capable girl indeed. Not only did she look after the apartment efficiently but she was also an excellent cook. But the best part of the time they spent together was in talking. Tom became closer to Shelley in those days than ever before.

He encouraged her to talk about home, knowing it would ease the parting for her.

'Didn't you have a boyfriend at home — Derek, wasn't it?' he asked one day. 'What will he do without you?'

'I liked him a lot, but I don't think we were destined for each other,' she said. 'If it's in the stars for us, he'll come out to Australia.'

'I see,' said Tom, a little taken aback.

Shelley threw a cushion at him, helpless with laughter. 'Oh, Dad, don't be such a square.'

He decided to invite Norrie Hampson and his wife Pat, for a meal. He was hopeful that Norrie might have found him a job by now. During the call, he told Norrie exactly what had happened between him and Joyce and the reason for Shelley's flight to Australia. Tom knew Pat would handle the situation with tact and tenderness.

He was right. Pat coped beautifully, not by trying to be a substitute mother for Shelley, but by treating her as an equal and discussing furnishings and decoration with her.

'Hey, what happened to you, man?'

Norrie said as they sat down to the meal. 'Most people come back from the Outback looking ten years older, not younger!'

'I guess the hard work put me in good shape again,' Tom said.

'I was amazed when I had that letter from you, what on earth were you doing on a cattle station?' Norrie asked.

'That's where I found Mrs Donnelly. I had to give her compensation money from the company and finally tracked her down in the Outback. When I got there, I found she and her dad were going through a sticky patch so I helped out doing odd jobs.'

'They'd be glad to get the money,' Norrie said.

Tom shrugged. 'She wouldn't take it. Pride, you know.'

This evening wasn't going the way he'd planned at all. He didn't want to talk about Whangiehill. Somehow, over the last few days the little family had been constantly in his thoughts and he had deliberately invited the Hampsons tonight to take his mind off the fact that today was the day the options ran out on the property. It was now three weeks since he'd left the cattle station. Today was the day of decision for Lisa and Chet.

'Dad,' Shelley nudged him, 'Uncle Norrie's saying he thinks he's found a job for you.'

'Oh, sorry. A job, that's great,' Tom tried to sound enthusiastic.

'It's only a preliminary interview so far, but I guess with your experience and your new look of health and vigour, you should be in with a shout,' Norrie said slowly.

'I'll do my best,' a thought struck Tom. 'Say, Norrie, have you any contact with freelance drilling teams?'

Norrie stared at him for a moment. 'I know how to rustle up one, if necessary.'

'It's a particular one I'm after. Mike Yarrow leads it, I guess it will go under his name. I reckon he'll be back in town in a few days.'

'I'll try to locate him,' his friend promised. 'Now about this job.'

'Sorry,' Tom apologized. 'I've been very rude.'

'No, worries, I'd say,' Norrie smiled. 'Anyway, call this number and arrange an interview. It's in Canberra. Just a six month consultancy contract, but if things go well, I reckon you'd find a place with them.'

After Pat and Norrie had gone, he helped Shelley with the washing up.

'Dad, wouldn't you rather go back to Whangiehill than find a job in Canberra?' she asked.

It took Tom a few moments to reply. 'There's nothing more I can do there, I just would like to know if Mike found water.'

'Was the situation desperate?'

'Yes.'

'And you really care, don't you?'

Tom turned to his daughter. He'd told her next to nothing about his weeks in Whangiehill, yet she must have sensed his concern.

He nodded. 'They were a brave little family,' he said.

Tom put off telephoning Canberra for an appointment on the pretext that it was now just a few days before Christmas. He took Shelley shopping and they decorated the apartment, just as if they were at home.

Two days before Christmas, Mike telephoned. He'd just arrived back in Sydney and found a message from Norrie to phone Tom.

Tom immediately invited him round to the apartment.

The sight of the stocky driller standing in the doorway, half an hour later, brought back a mixture of memories to Tom. The two men shook hands, but Tom didn't even have to ask the vital question.

'No joy, mate,' Mike said immediately.

Tom's heart sank. Poor Lisa, what rotten luck!

Shelley appeared from the kitchen with a tray of coffee cups.

'If only I could have persuaded Chet — ' Mike had continued speaking, but the appearance of Shelley stopped him in mid-flow.

The driller looked quite stunned. Tom turned to look at his daughter. For the first time he saw her as a stranger might. She was tall and really rather graceful; something he'd been unaware of before. Her fair hair was bleached by the Australian sun, and her skin had acquired an even golden tan, highlighting the clear blue of her eyes. Resemblance to Joyce was there in the regular features, but then she smiled and Tom recognized his own smile.

'Mike, this is my daughter, Shelley. Shelley meet Mike Yarrow,' he said.

'Pleased to meet you,' the warmth of Mike's voice underlined his words.

'Hi, come into the living room and have some coffee,' Shelley greeted him with the ease of youth, and led the way into the living room.

'Maybe you will tell me all about Whangiehill,' she said, handing Mike a cup of coffee. 'Dad has hardly said a word about it.'

Mike stirred his coffee.

'It's a sad business, Shelley. The cattle were desperate for water and we found none.'

'But surely there must be water somewhere?' Shelley protested.

'There's plenty underground, but finding it is the secret,' Mike said. 'I know I *would* have found it, given more time. Your dad was willing to put up extra money for more drilling but Chet and Lisa were too proud to accept.' He turned to Tom. 'I guess that's why you left so suddenly — you'd had enough.'

It took Tom a few moments to realize that Mike didn't know the real reason for his abrupt departure.

'I wish you'd stayed on,' Mike went on without waiting for Tom's confirmation. 'I finally got Chet to move to another location and I reckon I was within a few feet of water when the money ran out. I don't like to be beaten like that.'

'You just had to pack up and come home?' Shelley asked.

Mike shrugged. 'No alternative. I had to pay off my team,' he saw Tom's enquiring glance. 'The boys have gone to Queensland. Heard about some work there.'

'What's happening at Whangiehill now?' Tom could hardly bear to ask the question.

'It will take about a month for Chet to organize a muster, then drive the herd to whoever buys it.'

'What are they doing for water in the meantime?' Shelley asked.

'Matt Wylie is allowing Chet's herd to graze on his land for the next month on the eat now, pay later, principle,' Mike said to Tom.

Tom explained to Shelley about Matt being Chet's next-door neighbour, so to speak.

Mike helped himself to some of Shelley's cookies, complimenting her on her baking.

Tom had been doing some hard thinking.

'So they can stay on at Whangiehill for another month?' he asked Mike.

Mike nodded. 'Yeah, the mineral company is sending in a geologist to do some surveying.'

'That means there is another month left in which to find water?'

Mike stared at him.

'Technically yes, but Chet has no money and I have no team.'

Tom could feel excitement mounting inside him; maybe he could yet save Whangiehill.

'If I put up the money, could you find a team?'

Mike slowly put his coffee cup down on the table without looking, missing the saucer entirely.

'Are you serious, man?'

'Never more.'

Mike whooped with joy. 'What I'd give to find water on that property! I just know it's there,' he turned to Shelley. 'I hate leaving a job half-done.'

'So does dad,' she replied quietly.

'How will you square it with Chet

155

and Lisa?' Mike asked.

Tom shrugged. 'I'll think of something, like maybe offering to buy a share of the property.'

Mike got to his feet. 'I sure don't want to leave, but I must get a team together.'

'Are you alone in Sydney?' Tom asked him.

The driller nodded. 'My family live in Brisbane.'

'Then come to us on Christmas Day.'

Mike beamed at them. 'Thanks, that's a beaut idea.'

After Mike had gone, Shelley came into the living room and sat on the arm of Tom's chair.

'How about starting at the beginning and telling me all about Lisa Donnelly and Whangiehill, Dad. I know there's something worrying you.'

He realized that he owed Shelley a complete explanation, especially if he was going to put up some of his capital for the cattle station. He began the story right when he arrived at Whangiehill and told her everything. She listened in total silence until he finished. Then she slid her arm round his shoulders.

'We've got to do something for them, Dad. I don't know how, but you can't just leave things be. I feel responsible in a way. If I hadn't decided to fly out, Mum wouldn't have phoned and Lisa wouldn't have known — '

'No, my love, that part is all my fault, but we'll do something.'

★ ★ ★

Mike arrived on Christmas morning, loaded with gifts and food, but Tom could tell he wasn't completely relaxed.

'It's a bad time to raise a team, Tom,' being Mike he went straight to the heart of the matter. 'I've only managed to hire two old mates. You see, the ideal plan is to have a self-sufficient team, camp out on the site and work round the clock if necessary, particularly when time is short — as in this situation.'

Tom thought fast. He'd give anything

to be part of that team, but it would mean leaving Shelley in Sydney. He was reluctant to do that so soon after her arrival although he knew he could ask Pat and Norrie to put her up.

'Dad would love to be part of your team,' Shelley said quietly to Mike.

Tom's head turned in her direction. Had she read his thoughts?

'Sure like to have you along, Tom.'

'I wouldn't leave — '

'A team like that would need a cook, right, Mike?' Shelley went on.

'Too true.'

'Would you accept Dad as a crew member and me as cook?'

'Now, hold on a minute — ' Tom began.

Mike was struggling for an answer. 'I sure would like to have you both along, but the Outback is rough, Shelley.'

'Exactly, not the place for a girl,' Tom intersposed.

'Lisa Donnelly and her young daughter seem to have survived,' Shelley said coolly.

'That's different,' Tom said.

'It isn't going to be for long, because Mike's going to find water quickly, aren't you?' she smiled conspiratorily at Mike.

'Aw heck, Shelley, now I don't know what to say,' he said.

'As for my cooking — ' Shelley began to dish up dinner.

It took her to the end of Christmas Day to convince them, but once they realized how determined she was that both she and Tom should go, they started planning the trip.

The next few days were hectic, with Mike organizing the technical equipment, Tom hiring tents and other necessities, and Shelley learning to cope with enormous food supplies. Mike's two 'old mates', Rob and Barry, who turned out to be around thirty years of age, were a friendly and experienced pair.

Finally, on the last day of December, they were ready and set off just after dawn. Mike had hired two utility trucks, taking Tom and Shelley with him, while the others followed behind.

For the last few nights Tom had wrestled with the problem of calling Chet to ask permission to drill, but in the end decided that a surprise arrival on his doorstep might be of more value. Chet would find it more difficult to send away a drilling team already on site, so to speak, than to refuse by letter. Tom had no idea at all as to how Lisa would react.

As they drew nearer to Whangiehill, he began to wonder if he'd been too precipitate. He was interfering in their lives again, even if he meant well. Had he the right to do that?

The two trucks reached the Whangie-hill perimeter fence and went through the gate. Tom knew that the dust they raised would soon be seen at the homestead. He began to feel a little apprehensive about their reception. At the same time he found he was looking forward to seeing Lisa again. She'd been a real prickly customer, but he'd missed her in these last few weeks.

As they reached the homestead, he could see Chet and the children standing on the verandah.

'Leave this to me,' Tom said, and jumped down from the truck.

'Hi, stranger,' Chet greeted him.

Tom shook his hand.

'I thought you weren't ever coming back,' Neal levelled a fist at Tom's chest. 'You didn't even say goodbye.'

'He hadn't time, silly,' Kim told her brother. 'Mummy told you he had to get to Sydney quickly to meet his daughter. Hello, Tom,' she finished shyly.

'Hello Kim, hello Neal,' Tom smiled at the children, his heart somewhat lighter. So Lisa hadn't told the children the real reason for his departure. Did that mean she had forgiven him? It was now desperately important to him that she had.

'What you got there?' Chet was squinting at the two trucks.

'One complete self-sufficient drilling team.'

Chet turned to him and Tom saw the flare of hope in the old man's eyes.

'I'd like permission to drill for water on your land, Chet.'

'For what purpose?'

'I hear Whangiehill is up for sale, I could be interested.'

'If you don't find water, you don't buy?' Chet said warily.

'We'll find water,' Tom said.

He was knotted inside with tension and a strange excitement, hoping Chet would agree and wondering what Lisa would say. Where was she? He resisted an impulse to rush into the homestead looking for her.

Chet seemed to sag a little. 'You have my permission, Tom. I'm sure glad to see you and I hope to God you find water.'

'I'd like to square it with Lisa, too,' he said to Chet. 'Is she in the kitchen?'

He made to enter the homestead.

Chet's voice stopped him. 'Lisa isn't at Whangiehill, Tom. She's left.'

Tom's body was arrested in the dash

to the kitchen. She wasn't here! He felt all the fight, all the life, all the excitement drain out of him. As he turned to look at Chet and the children, he gradually realized why he'd come back to Whangiehill. To find water yes, to save the situation yes, but most of all to be with the woman he loved.

6

Tom's hand reached out for the verandah rail in an almost unconscious attempt to steady himself. He felt a tremendous sensation of disappointment at Lisa's absence, yet this was countered by the shock of the discovery of his feelings for her. He hadn't realized how fond of her he'd become.

'I know mummy would have liked to be here to greet you, Tom,' Kim's clear voice penetrated his thoughts.

He looked down at the child, startled to see that her assumed poise made her seem like a miniature replica of her mother.

'Won't you come in and have some tea?' she asked politely.

'Hey!' Neal's voice interrupted Tom's reply. 'There's a girl in the cab of that truck!' he sounded horrified.

'Is it Shelley?' Kim asked eagerly.

Chet was already walking over to the lead truck, giving Mike a friendly greeting. Soon everyone was crowding onto the homestead verandah, the sturdy drillers dwarfing the children.

'Can I help you, Kim?' Shelley asked as the girl went along the passage to the kitchen.

Kim turned and nodded shyly. Tom had noticed her eyes drinking in every detail of Shelley, from the thick fair hair, now released from the cover of her bush hat, to the everyday Outback gear of shirt and jeans and leather boots. Nothing glamorous, but it had to be admitted that Shelley had style and Kim was enchanted.

The men settled themselves on the verandah chairs and the chat was joking and easy. Tom had been worried that Chet might be resentful of Mike's presence on the station again reminding him of the unsuccessful bid to find water, but the old man warmly welcomed everyone.

Tom's eyes lingered a little longer on

Chet. He had aged since they last met and Tom was shocked at the difference. Chet looked very tired and Tom suspected that he'd had enough tribulation at Whangiehill.

'It was Lisa's idea to find a new owner for Whangiehill, with the condition that I manage the station,' he told Tom.

'How is she financing the trip?' Tom was blunt. They were speaking quietly at their end of the verandah while Neal amused the drillers with some wild stories.

'Using her own nest egg; now there's nothing left for her future,' Chet said. 'She hasn't touched the children's money. I told her not to do this. There's no point in being at Whangiehill unless it's ours.'

Tom didn't reply, but he could see Lisa's reasoning. If she did find a new owner who was willing to let them stay on, they would still have a home for Kim and Neal. He guessed Lisa was desperate not to uproot the children again in such a short time.

'Why didn't the mineral company move in right away?'

'Search me,' Chet rolled a cigarette. 'First they pushed the bank to put a time limit on the sale date, then they said they wanted some surveys carried out before the deal goes through.'

'It's working out in our favour,' Tom pointed out. 'Giving us a month's grace.'

Chet sighed. 'Maybe you'll find water.'

There was a hint of hopelessness in his voice and from his choice of words, Tom realized that Chet would not be helping out this time. The old man had already given his all to Whangiehill.

After a meal, jointly prepared and served by Shelley and Kim, Tom took a walk by himself around the homestead buildings. He was surprised to find how much affinity he felt with the place; he hadn't realized how involved he'd become with Whangiehill. Still, there was a great sense of emptiness about

the place that was simply summed up
— no Lisa.

Tom thought back to the reasons
he'd given Shelley for Joyce and Alan
falling in love. No doubt the same thing
had happened here. Two people thrown
together in times of stress and the
admiration he'd initially felt for Lisa
had grown into love. But there the
similarity stopped. He was certain
Lisa's feelings for him were quite
different. Anyway, he must be at least
ten years older than her.

He kicked a stone, raising a cloud of
dust. He may never be anything to Lisa
Donnelly, but at least he could do
everything in his power to make life a
little better for her.

Then he ran into Banka and was
warmed to see the friendly greeting on
the Aborigine's face.

'Tom, I'm glad you've come back.
Whangiehill needs you.'

The two men shook hands. Banka
seemed to accept Tom's surprise return
without question.

'I've brought Mike and a drilling team,' Tom told him. 'I intend to find water in the next four weeks.'

Banka beamed. 'Good. Then I can stay at Whangiehill, too.'

'Perhaps you can help us find water,' Tom said thinking that he might know of some tribal watering holes.

But Tom was disappointed.

Banka shook his head. 'All the old watering holes have dried up,' he shrugged. 'Like the creek.'

It took Tom a few moments to assimilate what Banka had said. All was completely quiet; night had come to Whangiehill, the birds were silent and the moon eerily illuminated the station and its empty arid acres.

'A creek?' Tom at last managed to get the word out. 'You mean there was once a creek here at Whangiehill?'

Banka nodded. 'I reckon so from the look of the ground. Over there,' he pointed to the west of the hill that gave the station its name.

'Show me,' Tom hurried the Aborigine

over the hard-baked ground.

'All dried up now,' Banka said fifteen minutes later as he and Tom stood looking at a wide but shallow trench that circled the west flank of the hill. Tom hadn't given the area a second look when he'd been at the station before. Of course, he didn't have Banka's sharp huntsman eyes.

'The water came from somewhere over there,' Banka waved a hand at a group of rocks some distance away. Moonlight was deceptive and Tom couldn't even hazard a guess at to the position of the rocks in terms of mileage from the homestead.

'All dried up — long time ago,' Banka shook his head sagely.

Tom looked again at the trench. If there once had been enough water here to form a creek it must have come from an underground river, or perhaps even a tributary of a river. That indicated a good flow of water. From talks with Mike about the Great Artesian Basin, Tom knew that plenty of water ran beneath the surface land. This outlet may have dried up or been cut off for many reasons. It was very possible, though, that the original river was still there, under those rocks.

If only they'd known about this before. He couldn't blame Banka. No one had asked his advice and from his comments it was obvious that he didn't realize there might be more water from the same source. Banka wandered off and Tom hurried back to the homestead.

Mike was excited and optimistic about Tom's news.

'It's too dark tonight to make a proper survey, but we'll go out at first light tomorrow,' he said to Tom. 'This is every driller's dream, to find water which would give a permanent supply to a cattle station. To think that there once was water so near to the homestead! If we can re-create the situation, Tom, we can channel water right down here, as well as to the grazing lands. This place might never go dry again.'

Mike woke him a few hours later, just as dawn was breaking. Chet had loaned the team two of his horses and they rode out, their hopes high.

In the harsh light of day, the rocks proved to be a good fifteen miles from the homestead. The two men started off at the creek bed and were amazed to find what had been the course of a river now leading back to the rocks. It was easy to identify, although years of dust storms had disguised it to the casual eye.

'This must have been dried up long before Chet came to Whangiehill,' Mike said. 'He obviously knew nothing about it.'

The rocks covered a large area and proved to be an odd assortment of huge slabs and strange pinnacles obviously eroded by the elements over millions of years.

'Man, have we got ourselves some drilling here,' Mike pushed the bush hat to the back of his head as he surveyed the rocks.

'Seems to me we could drill for weeks and still not hit the right spot,' Tom said, his spirits low.

'I'll make some random test bores first,' Mike said decisively. 'After all, we know there must be water here somewhere. On the other site, we were just drilling with optimism and not much else.'

They spent the rest of the day moving between the site and the homestead organizing the trucks and the gear. With Mike in charge of operations, the tents were erected first, then the drilling gear set up.

Tom kept a close eye on Shelley. This whole set-up, the country, the climate, everything was alien to her. She worked on doggedly, unpacking the supplies which she'd bought on Mike's instructions, and then concocted a meal. It was no dainty meat and two veg for the team either, but gargantuan portions of steak and mounds of potatoes and bread.

The days began to fall into a pattern

of work. Mike constantly had Tom and the men move the drilling rig from test site to test site. Tom was glad that he'd had time to build up his strength during the previous stay at Whangiehill. He would never have stood the pace of the hard manual work otherwise.

As the days passed, his admiration for his daughter grew. The novelty of the camp, the new job, had surely worn off, but still she was cheerful and thoughtful to him and the men, always anticipating when they were desperate for a cold beer and some extra 'tucker'.

Sometimes, in the evening when it was cool, Mike took her riding. Although first attracted by Shelley's appearance and personality, it was obvious that he was also impressed by her strength of character. His brief comments of 'Good on you, Shelley,' held respect and admiration.

When he was alone, Tom thought constantly of Lisa, and wondered if she'd returned home. If so, he'd seen nothing of her and it disturbed him to think she might be keeping out of his way.

About a week after they'd begun drilling, Tom spotted a cloud of dust approaching from the direction of the homestead, indicating a visitor approaching. His heart raced at the thought it could be Lisa coming to see them at last.

He was horrified when he saw it was Neal, on his own. Tom left the rig and ran over to where the boy was riding his horse into the small corral they'd erected for Chet's two horses.

'What's happened, Neal? Why are you here on your own?'

'Nothing's happened,' Neal slid off his saddle nonchalantly. 'I just came out to see how things were going.'

'Chet let you ride out alone?' Tom was astounded. No children ever went out alone in the Outback. Any accident could occur and the fierce sun could dehydrate an injured person in a short time.

'He wasn't around when I left,' Neal said carelessly.

'Does Kim know you're here?' Tom didn't think Kim would have given Neal permission to ride out, but the boy might have ignored her refusal.

'Can I work the drill, Mike? Will you show me?' Neal made to run across to the drill platform, but Tom caught his arm and roughly pulled him back to stand in front of him.

'Not only have you ridden out here alone, but you haven't told anyone you were coming, have you?' he demanded.

Neal shrugged. 'I can take care of myself.'

'Nobody can take care of himself alone in the Outback.'

Neal shuffled his feet, causing minor dust clouds.

'What about your mother?' Tom asked.

'She isn't home yet.'

'So you think it's okay to walk out on your chores at the homestead and act irresponsibly in doing just what you want?' Tom knew his words were a bit strong for an eight-year-old but he had to make him see the dangers.

'Don't you realize that your mother went away thinking she could trust you not only to behave sensibly but also to look out for Kim and your grandfather, as they look out for you? If you had got lost, how would an old man and a girl know where to begin to search for you out here? Living on a cattle station is team work, don't you think, Neal?'

The boy's face had a mulish set to it.

'First of all,' Tom told him. 'You will see to your horse, then you will ask Shelley for a drink and something to eat, then we'll ride straight back to the homestead.'

'Aw Tom,' Neal began.

'Now!' Tom bellowed.

Neal slouched across to his horse without another look at Tom.

Thirty minutes later, Tom and the boy rode out of the drilling camp site and headed for the cattle station. As they approached the homestead Tom could see Kim standing on the

177

verandah. She ran down the steps towards them.

'Oh, Tom, I'm so glad to see you. I thought Neal — ' the words stopped and she began to cry.

'It's okay, Kim. He's all right.'

Without being asked Neal took the reins of both horses and led them off to the corral. Tom took the still trembling Kim into the kitchen of the homestead and made some strong coffee.

'Grandad is out with Banka, checking on our herd over on Matt Wylie's land, and I didn't know where Neal had gone,' she told Tom.

'I can assure you, Kim, he'll never do anything like that again,' Tom put a mug of coffee in front of her.

By the time she'd finished the coffee, Kim had calmed down again, but there was still a look of anxiety about her face. Tom felt concerned that she and Neal were still on their own and decided to stay at the homestead until Chet's return.

A few moments later Neal came into the kitchen.

'I'm sorry, Kim, I shouldn't have gone off like that. I won't do it again,' then he turned to Tom. 'I want to say sorry to you, too, Tom. I was real stupid.'

It was an enormous apology for a small boy to make and Tom guessed it had cost him a lot.

'I guess everyone is allowed one big mistake and I think you're clever enough not to make another one,' Tom said gently.

Neal looked a little cheered by Tom's comments.

'Tell you what, I'll come in the truck in say a couple of days' time and take you and Kim on a proper visit to the camp. We'll get Shelley to knock up a feast or something.'

'Oh, great!' Neal's natural exhuberance began to return. 'I really do want to know about drilling.'

There was a noise from outside the front of the homestead, just like a car door closing. The children looked at each other, hope in their faces.

'Do you think it could be mum?' Kim asked.

Then they raced out of the kitchen. Tom heard their whoops of joy and Lisa's laugh. She was here.

He stood in the kitchen, undecided what to do. He could hardly slip out of the back door and ride back to the camp, the children would be bound to tell Lisa he'd been here. Yet he was unsure of coping with Lisa's reaction when she saw him.

Then Neal came through the kitchen door like a tornado, shouting — 'Look who's here, Mum!'

Lisa came in, a look of polite expectancy on her face.

'Hello, Lisa,' he said quietly.

'Tom . . . ,' she flushed a little. 'Hello,' her eyes quickly left his face and she put her bag on the kitchen chair.

Well, at least she hadn't thrown him out, or even looked angry, Tom thought, his heart hammering at the sight of her again.

Before he could say anything, Neal told Lisa exactly why Tom had come back to Whangiehill and all about Shelley, Mike and the drillers.

'I wanted your permission to drill as well as Chet's,' Tom said. 'But there wasn't time to wait until your return.'

She nodded. 'I understand. It's okay by me,' her voice was almost without inflexion and for one awful moment, Tom thought she didn't care one way or another what happened.

'Did you find a buyer?'

She looked at him with a wry smile. 'No water, no buyer.'

Tom tried to keep his expression non-committal but he couldn't help feeling glad. Had Lisa found a buyer, he, Mike and the others would have had to pack up and leave. That was the last thing he wanted.

Lisa looked exhausted, and defeated. Quickly he poured her some coffee and Kim, quick to notice too, began to take some salad from the fridge.

After the meal, Lisa began to relax a

little and asked Tom about Shelley. He told her briefly what had happened since he'd left Whangiehill. Their conversation was a little stilted as both were conscious of their last confrontation at the homestead.

However, Lisa's interest came alive again when he told her about the dry creek bed and Mike's conviction that there was plenty of water somewhere under the rocks.

'If only we'd asked Banka before,' she said to Tom.

'Banka had knowledge he didn't know about,' Tom shrugged, then stood up. There was no necessity for him to stay until Chet returned now.

'I'd better get back to the camp.'

'We'll get your horse ready, Tom,' Neal and Kim offered, running outside.

Tom picked up his hat. He didn't think Lisa would want him hanging around any longer, but her voice stopped him at the door.

'Tom — Bill *was* driving that day, wasn't he?' He could hardly hear her.

He turned towards the table and put down his hat.

'Yes.'

'Did you have a special car or something? I know he was crazy about different models.'

'It was a Rover, he hadn't driven one before.'

She nodded, still not looking at Tom.

'I would never have given him the wheel if it hadn't been one of those unexpectedly lovely February days,' Tom said. 'It was cold, but clear, sunny even, with a few odd clouds.'

She turned to him, her eyes puzzled. 'Then what happened? Bill was a good driver.'

Tom nodded. 'The best, better than me. It's difficult to explain if you don't know England's climate. One minute clear sky, the next dense fog, no warning. This happens particularly in the industrial areas. It happened that day. Even then, Bill coped magnificently. The driver overtaking us didn't.

He didn't see the lorry directly in front of him until it was too late. He cut in on Bill who swerved to avoid a crash — but he had no chance.'

Lisa was now sitting opposite him, staring at her hands on the table.

'I didn't want to believe he was driving, I wanted to blame someone else. Perhaps it was being so far away from it all that made it unreal. I waved Bill off at Sydney airport and never saw him again. He's even buried in England,' she paused. 'This must sound crazy to you.'

'No,' he said. 'I understand now. I didn't when I first met you, but now I can see it from this side of the world, as it were.'

'Bill's death must have seemed so pointless,' he said after a moment. 'I suppose that's why I didn't tell you the truth that day I first arrived here. I felt you couldn't take any more at that time.'

For the first time Lisa looked straight at him.

'I did a lot of thinking while I was away from Whangiehill,' she said after a while. 'Somehow I couldn't believe that you'd set out to deceive me and I began to face up to the real facts.'

Tom said nothing but he wondered if she'd ever realize how much it meant to him to know that she didn't think he'd deliberately deceived her.

'Why were you so insistent that I take the money, Tom?' she asked.

'I suppose I felt I'd let Bill down. You see, Lisa, even after I'd come out of that long coma, I didn't remember about Bill at all. I remembered nothing about the crash. My memory had so many blanks at first. Then one day all the pieces came together and . . . and I learned what had happened to Bill. I was horrified that the company hadn't heard from you and hadn't followed up their first letter.'

'But you didn't come out to Australia just to see me, surely?'

'No,' he said, and determined that there would be no secrets from Lisa in future, he told her everything about Joyce and Alan.

'You lost someone, too, as a result of the crash. I'm sorry, Tom,' she said softly.

'Like you, I have come to terms with my life now. Shelley has joined me here and we've decided to stay in Australia.'

'Really?' Lisa looked very surprised. 'Isn't it a bit risky to put your money in Whangiehill then?'

He shrugged. 'When I heard there was a last chance to find water, I just had to act. It seemed an awful waste for Chet's work to go for nothing if he had to lose the station. I know what it's like to create something, Lisa. Alan Markham and I built up our business from scratch, half on credit, half on sheer nerve. I don't want the company now, but I'd hate to see it disappear.'

Lisa nodded slowly, obviously weighing up what he'd said.

'Let's hope you're successful here then,' she said in a neutral tone of voice.

Tom left soon after, happy that Lisa was home again, but also with a sensation of emptiness. She hadn't said she was glad he'd returned or that she appreciated his efforts to save Whangiehill. In fact, she had been quite distant with him in a way. They'd been friends before, but now they seemed to have lost that easy relationship, even although she'd admitted she had been wrong about him.

It took Tom a long time to ride back to camp and his spirits were low as he dismounted from his horse and led it to the corral. He wasn't aware of the silence at first, then he realized the drill wasn't operating.

He quickly walked out of the corral and saw Mike striding towards him. Shelley and the two drillers were standing by the mess tent, watching Mike.

'Hey, catch this,' Mike shouted, throwing something at Tom.

Tom's reactions were slow and the missile landed on his shoulder with a 'splat'!

'Yeugh, what's that?' Tom scraped bits of mud off his shirt. Then his eyes widened as he realized the significance.

'Mud?' he whispered, then looked up at Mike. 'Mud!' he exclaimed this time. 'This is from the bore?'

'Yep,' Mike's grin was a mile wide. 'And mud means water.'

'Hallelujah!' cried Tom.

Shelley and the drillers came over and they all talked excitedly for a few moments.

'I think this calls for a celebration,' Tom said.

'Hold on a bit,' Mike said cautiously, 'that could be a little premature. We haven't discovered the source yet, although we must be near it. But I do reckon we deserve a break.'

It was while the little group were laughing and joking over beer and some cookies which Shelley had managed to bake, that they saw the now familiar cloud of dust heralding a visitor.

'Small truck, or the like,' Mike said, squinting in the distance, 'and not coming from the direction of the homestead.'

It was a jeep, new and dusty, but otherwise in top condition.

The man who stepped down from it looked in much the same class. He brushed the dust from a safari style outfit which was more expensive than Tom had ever seen around the Outback. His boots were of the finest leather. The man himself was fairly tall with dark hair and a lean, aristocratic looking face, good cheek bones, longish nose and firm mouth. It was hard to tell his age and at best Tom could only guess at somewhere between twenty-eight and thirty-eight. He approached the group with a friendly and confident smile.

'Good day to you,' he said. 'Desmond Corby, geologist with the mining company interested in this property.'

'I'm Tom Price and this is Mike Yarrow in charge of the drilling team,' Tom also introduced Rob, Barrie and Shelley.

Desmond Corby genially shook hands with everyone.

'Just packing up are you?' he asked.

'No,' Tom stared at the younger man.

'But there's no water on this property,' Corby said.

'Who told you that?' Mike asked.

'I've just come from Matt Wylie's place. He told me that Chet Oliphant's cattle are grazing on his land.'

'Temporarily,' Tom said.

'Wylie said the drilling operation was finished,' there was an edge to Corby's voice.

'I've set up a new one,' Tom said.

Desmond Corby's face seemed to narrow a little.

'My company knows nothing about this,' he said.

'Why should it? Whangiehill isn't their property — yet.' For some reason he couldn't define Tom was rapidly taking a dislike to Desmond Corby.

The narrow eyes were sharp, too, as they took in the damp patch on Tom's shirt and the lumps of mud sitting like trophies on the centre of the picnic table.

'I guess Whangiehill is big enough to accommodate us all while we search for whatever nature has hidden underground,' Mike spoke up.

Corby's eye roamed over the strange formation of rocks at the site.

'I won't be working here, anyway,' he said.

'Will you have some beer and cookies, Mr Corby?' Shelley offered.

Instantly the lean face changed expression and became strikingly handsome.

'That's very civil of you, Miss Price.'

Tom and Mike exchanged a quick glance. They both knew Shelley had taken some of the tension out of the situation, which was a good thing. They weren't in a position to antagonize any potential buyer for Whangiehill. After all, mud was mud, it wasn't a river.

A rather uneasy truce existed between Corby and the drilling team over the next few days. He dropped

191

in at the camp at least once each day, ostensibly as a friendly visit, but Tom suspected he was anxious to know how successful the drilling was proving.

Tom could barely speak he was so frustrated. Oh, they'd found a source of water, a pathetic little trickle, nothing more.

Somehow Corby had wangled a room at Chet's homestead and was riding out each day to make his surveys.

'You know that guy is probably reporting to Lisa and Chet every night, not only about his own findings, but ours, too,' Mike said one evening as they sat despondently in the mess tent.

'I expect so,' Tom said, without much interest.

'Don't you see he has the edge on us?' Mike said.

Tom looked enquiringly at the driller, not following his line of talk.

'If he can jump the gun by saying he has found a good lode somewhere and offers Chet a smashing price for

Whangiehill, we could be wasting our time.'

'But the drilling isn't costing Chet anything,' Tom said.

'Maybe not, but the grazing is costing Lisa,' Mike said patiently. 'If Corby offers a good price, she may feel obliged to insist that Chet takes it, on account of the kids.'

'I don't think — '

'Don't be naïve, Tom. That Corby is one sharp operator, I can tell. Now I know we're gonna hit a big river under these rocks, but I don't know when. The thing is you must tell Lisa we need an even chance with Corby. Please, Tom, go and see her.'

Tom considered Mike's suggestion. In a way he was reluctant to return to the homestead in the face of Lisa's cool reception last time. Then he remembered that he'd promised to bring Kim and Neal to the camp for the day.

'O.K. I'll go first thing tomorrow,' he said. 'I don't think we should mention this to Corby.'

'Too right,' Mike said grimly.

Next day, Tom had a rousing welcome from Kim and Neal and then they raced off to finish their chores before leaving with him. He'd come in one of the trucks as Shelley needed some more supplies which Chet had stored at the homestead for her.

'Come and have some coffee when you've finished loading,' Lisa called from the kitchen door.

When he'd finished, he went inside the house, his eyes drinking in the sight of this attractive girl. She looked especially lovely today, a blouse of dusty pink enhancing her fair hair and clear eyes. She'd had her hair cut while away from Whangiehill and the style suited her, its luxuriant thickness curving softly round her face.

'Any luck?' she asked him.

'A few streams, but nothing like enough water at the moment to be of any real use.'

'But you've actually found some water, that's marvellous!' she was astonished and Tom realized that Corby must have said nothing to her about their progress.

'I've been thinking about you and wondering how you were faring in the camp,' she said.

Tom's spirits rose. She hadn't forgotten him and she did care about them out there among the rocks.

'It must be really hard on Shelley in this strange environment, doing all that cooking,' Lisa said with warmth and sympathy.

'To tell you the truth, Lisa, I never thought she'd stick it, but she has and I'm really proud of her,' he said.

They sat for almost fifteen minutes, just chatting. For Tom it was just like old times, and yet it was better. Everything was open and honest between them now, there was nothing to hinder a closer friendship. Gradually he brought the conversation round to the water situation again and, although he was sure now that Lisa would not hastily sell out to the mining company, he decided to do the right thing and ask her to promise. He didn't get the chance.

'Well, good day to you, Tom!'

Tom froze in his chair at the sound of Desmond Corby's voice behind him.

'Morning, Des, kept some breakfast for you,' Lisa said, smiling over Tom's head.

Tom swung round in his chair.

'Thought you would have been out on your surveys long before this,' he said, unable to keep the sharpness from his voice.

Corby slid into another chair at the table and yawned noticeably.

'Late night. We sat up talking, didn't we, Lisa? Reckon it was the small hours before we got to bed,' he grinned at Tom.

Tom was looking at Lisa, but she was standing at the cooker, frying bacon, her back to the two men. She didn't answer.

Tom rose. 'I'd better see if the children are ready.'

'Found another Nile yet?' Corby said sarcastically.

Tom kept his temper in check with the greatest difficulty. 'We're not expecting miracles,' he paused. 'Perhaps, of course, the land is rich with minerals.'

Corby's head swung round to look at Tom and his expression was sharp.

'We should be so lucky! There's nothing out there,' he glanced quickly at Lisa's back. 'Nothing worth mining yet anyway, surface stuff only.'

'But you'll keep trying,' Tom said.

'I never give up,' Corby looked at him levelly, 'on anything.'

Tom left the homestead in a turmoil of anger and frustration. Things had been going so well between him and Lisa until Corby had walked in. Tom felt the whole careful reconstruction of their earlier relationship had just crumbled again.

Kim and Neal climbed into the cab truck beside him and he started the engine. Lisa had come out on to the veranda to wave them off. Just before they moved off, Corby came out to join Lisa. Very deliberately he put an arm round her shoulders.

Tom was too far away to see the expression on Lisa's face, but she didn't move away from Corby.

Tom dragged his eyes away and turned the truck in the direction of the camp. Was there any point in going on? Was he going to lose Whangiehill and Lisa, too?

7

'I thought you would have learned to make bread properly by this time!'

'I thought you would have learned by this time that bread should not be left lying around uncovered. Of course it goes stale.'

'So we have only stale bread. Do we starve?'

'Not when I'm cook. I'll bake another batch.'

Tom was lying on his camp bed in his tent but he couldn't help overhearing the argument between Mike and Shelley. For a moment there was a charged silence outside, then Mike spoke again.

'Sorry, Shell — '

'Me, too,' Tom heard his daughter say.

'Guess I'm bushed,' Mike again.

'The heat's a bit much today,' Shelley admitted.

However, Tom knew that the real reason for the petty squabbles was failure; failure to find water. The situation was getting on everyone's nerves. They had been camped out by the rock formations for almost three weeks now. More than once they'd found sources of water. Even now the pump was working full time and water was being channelled to revitalize pasture for the cattle, but it still was not enough. The sources were meagre and the team had no idea just when the water might dry up again. The prize, the big river which Mike was convinced ran under the rocks somewhere, still eluded them.

Suddenly restless, Tom got up and left his tent. Outside Shelly and Mike were sitting at the table, having a cool drink. They weren't speaking, but Tom sensed a peaceful rapport between them again.

He shaded his eyes from the ever-present glare of the sun and, narrowing his eyes, scanned the horizon. There was no sign of Desmond Corby. Not the first time, Tom reflected that he found it surprising Corby had not yet found anything worth mining on the property.

He still hadn't been able to banish the memory of Lisa and Corby standing close together on the verandah of Whangiehill. Despite his dream to save the cattle station for Lisa, he was very much aware that Corby could have much more to offer her in the way of a good price for Whangiehill — and perhaps even marriage as well.

His thoughts were cut off abruptly as he spotted a rider approaching. Corby, he thought sourly, and probably with news of a successful survey. Jealousy and disappointment rose up in his throat again and he turned back into his tent.

It wasn't Corby who rode into camp though, but Banka; a serious, worried Banka. Tom went out to meet him.

'Chet is sick,' he told Tom, as the

drilling team clustered round to hear the news.

'Has the Flying Doctor seen him?'

'He'll be at the homestead soon, but I think you should come now, Tom,' Banka said.

'Did Lisa send you to fetch me?'

Banka shook his head. 'I know she needs you there,' he insisted.

Tom was hesitant. Lisa probably hadn't even thought of him. Although he knew Banka relied on him, he couldn't exactly barge in uninvited. Mike caught his eye and signalled he wanted a private word with him. They walked away from the group towards the tents.

'I think you should go,' Mike said.

'It sounds as if Lisa can cope, I don't want to push my nose in,' Tom really longed to go to the homestead, wanted to be by Lisa's side in any crisis, but he knew he was needed at the drilling site, too.

'Don't forget that Banka is an Aborigine tribesman, a different race, a different culture. They treat illness in an entirely different way,' Mike said. 'Maybe Lisa could do with someone to talk to.'

'Corby will be there,' Tom pointed out.

'Well, he must be somewhere,' Mike said, with heavy sarcasm. 'I never knew a geologist to survey in such an invisible way. I thought he would have been getting under our feet every day, trying to make some bores here,' he waved at the unusual rock formation around them.

'I admit I am worried about Chet,' Tom said. 'Maybe if I just went to the homestead for a couple of hours.'

'Stay overnight,' Mike advised. 'Don't ride back here in the dark. Don't worry about Shelley, we'll take good care of her, you can be sure of that.'

Tom smiled at the young driller. There was no doubting the sincerity and devotion in his voice, despite the earlier squabble.

Tom and Banka rode out of camp a

little later. It didn't take too long to cover the fifteen miles to the homestead. Before reaching it, however, they saw the Flying Doctor's aircraft heading back to Gillieston. Tom caught Banka's eye but he merely nodded. Tom guessed that Banka cared deeply for Chet, but didn't know how to express his concern in words.

The men rode into a subdued welcome from the children. Tom was cheered to see the relief on Lisa's face when he appeared. Banka had been right; she did need him. He hurried up the steps of the verandah.

'How is Chet? Has he been taken to hospital?'

Lisa shook her head. 'The doc's not sure what's wrong with dad. He thought he would be better at home, than hundreds of miles away alone in a hospital. Dad's . . . he's just lying in bed, Tom, saying nothing, doing nothing. He looks as if he isn't even thinking anything,' her voice broke a little on the last sentence.

'Hey, steady now,' Tom said very softly, putting an arm around her shoulder. 'He'll be okay. What exactly did the doc say?'

She shrugged. 'He was really puzzled. Just said to keep dad well fed, give him plenty of fluids, and talk to him.'

She opened the door of Chet's room and they went in together.

It looked as if Chet had been propped up in bed, then slid down any old how. His eyes were open but they didn't seem to register the fact that two people had entered the room.

Tom walked to the foot of the bed where he was in Chet's line of vision.

'Hi, Chet, what's all this then?' he said in a cheerful voice.

Chet's eyelids flickered and after a moment he said: 'Tom.' It was a flat, dull sound.

Tom couldn't diagnose his physical state, but he recognized his mental condition at once. The old man was giving up on life. Tom knew that defeated, exhausted look. He'd seen and known himself like that in those dark days just after he'd come out of hospital. At that time, he'd been convinced no one wanted him, or cared for him and that life was over. If a person thought there was nothing to live for, it was so easy to slide into total dejection.

'I'm going to make some tea for us all. Will you come and help?' Lisa asked.

Tom left the bedroom, knowing Lisa wanted his opinion right away.

'What do you think, Tom?' she asked as soon as they reached the kitchen.

He hesitated for a moment, then decided to give her the truth; he knew she could take it, hard though it would be.

'He's given up, Lisa. He feels he's failed you and the children, and there's no more fight left in him. He doesn't ever want to leave Whangiehill. He couldn't bear to live anywhere else.'

'You mean . . . he just wants to die here?' she whispered.

'He *thinks* he wants to die here,' Tom corrected gently. 'We have to see that he doesn't.'

'How, Tom — *how*?'

'First of all, I'll do something I should have been doing all along — bring him up to date on the progress of our drilling. I've been very selfish, Lisa, hoping to surprise Chet with news of discovering a big river, you know I wanted to appear the big hero, saving your station at the eleventh hour. I'm sorry about that, I just wanted to impress Chet and most of all, you.'

He saw surprise and then a glimmer of understanding dawning in her eyes.

He hurried on quickly, 'I haven't told him or you that we have found water, not enough to keep the station viable for your whole herd, but it is a beginning. We have to re-kindle hope in your dad, that's the only way to keep him alive.'

'Tom, I've been trying.'

'I know you have, but it needs someone who's out there, working on the rig,' Tom explained. 'Someone who is in the thick of things, making things happen,' he paused for a moment. He was reluctant to make the next admission, but he knew he had to be absolutely fair to Chet and Lisa. 'Desmond Corby might have some good news for Chet, too. Why don't you ask him to speak to Chet?'

Lisa shook her head. 'Desmond says he's finding surface lodes only. I don't reckon that's too good news for Dad.'

She poured out the tea.

'Would it be all right if I stayed over tonight?' Tom asked. 'Then I could have a good long talk with Chet.'

She turned her head and he saw a mixture of hope and appreciation in her expression.

'Of course, Tom. You know you are welcome in this house any time.'

That first evening Tom got no response at all from Chet. He gave him the facts about the drilling operations, not hiding the truth about the meagre sources, but being encouraging about finding a river. Chet made no comment at all and Tom wasn't even sure if he heard him. Eventually the old man fell asleep and Tom went out on to the verandah to join Lisa.

She talked a lot to Tom, mainly about the children and Tom listened, now and then giving advice or comment. Tom was glad he'd come for her sake, too, as she did need someone to talk to.

When they finished a late snack and rose to leave the verandah, Tom commented: 'Corby is very late tonight. Surely he can't still be surveying?'

'He doesn't sleep here every night,' Lisa told him. 'If he's working on a location near our border with some other property, he'll stay overnight there. He quite often takes a bed in Matt Wylie's bunkhouse.'

Although good news from Corby might have helped Chet, Tom was glad he hadn't had to suffer the man's company.

Tom was ready to leave next morning by sun-up.

'I'll come back again this evening,' he told Lisa. 'Try not leave him alone for long spells. I know it's difficult when you only have Banka to help out, but we must start your dad thinking and hoping again.'

'Tom, you've been a tremendous comfort. I . . . ,' Lisa paused. 'I'll look forward to seeing you again this evening.'

'Keep your spirits up, you're not alone,' he told her.

The children gave him a brief wave as he rode off. He'd already had a private word with them, asking them to double their chores, if possible, to give their mother more time to spend with Chet. The children, quiet and thoughtful, agreed at once. Tom rode out of the homestead, hoping and praying that there would be a good time ahead for those two. They were having to grow up too fast in this situation.

When he reached the camp, Shelley came running over to him, for once her pretty face drawn and anxious.

'It's okay, love, Chet isn't too bad,' he reassured her.

'Well, I'm glad *you* have good news,' she said. 'You'd better come over to the supplies tent.'

Inside the tent, the ground was covered with a huge mound of white. Tom went closer to inspect.

'Flour and sugar, tea as well over here,' Shelley ran the toe of her boot through a heap of tea leaves, which Tom hadn't noticed on the shadowy floor.

The remains of the large catering bags, split wide open, were piled on one side.

'What happened?'

'We don't know. I was last in here around sundown yesterday. Everything was fine then. When I came in this morning — this,' she shrugged. 'We left it for you to see. Mike says the vibration from the pump might have caused the boards to tilt.'

Tom looked round the supplies tent. The food was stored on shelves which slotted into free-standing uprights, and

211

the dry goods had been kept on the top shelves to be as far away as possible from any marauding wild life that might penetrate the tent.

Tom stretched out a hand and tested the uprights. They seemed pretty firm, as they'd been sunk into the ground a little for more support. Still he didn't know enough about a drilling operation to question Mike's theory.

'I'm sorry, Dad, maybe I didn't stack the bags on the shelves properly. We'll have to replace these stores and it will be so expensive.'

He put his arm round Shelley.

'Hey, don't take on so, it doesn't matter. We can afford it,' he told her.

'Someone will have to go to Gillieston to fetch them,' she pointed out.

That meant a whole day lost, Tom realized. A whole day for a crew member to be away was a real loss to the operation.

Later, he told Mike about Chet's condition.

'He needs someone to talk to him, to

keep him going, all the time. It's too much for Lisa to cope with. Would you mind if I took the evening shifts off and rode in to see him then?'

'That's okay by me,' Mike readily agreed.

'That's rotten luck about the supplies, Mike.'

'Sure is,' Mike's voice was grim.

'Should we move the site of the tent, if you think the vibration could cause this again?'

Mike was quiet for a moment. 'That was only one possible explanation, Tom.'

'Could it have been some animal?'

'That's possible, too,' Mike slowly rolled a cigarette. 'But there are no tracks,' he paused, then lit his cigarette. 'Look, Tom, why don't you take the truck into Gillieston tomorrow, fetch the supplies and call in on Chet on the way back? Take Shelley with you. She's blaming herself for this accident and it certainly isn't her fault. I reckon she needs a break from the camp, she hasn't had a day off since we arrived.'

Tom had privately thought that Shelley needed a break, too, but hadn't wanted to suggest depleting the team further, even for a day.

He and Shelley set out at sun-up next day. He had suggested to her that she might like to spend the day with Lisa and the children while he went into Gillieston. Lisa hadn't met her yet and he was anxious that they should get acquainted.

Kim and Neal gave Shelley a boisterous reception and Lisa welcomed her to Whangiehill with genuine warmth. Tom stood by and saw the girl and the woman take one long look at each other and noticed that each liked what they saw.

After a quick cup of coffee, Tom set off for Gillieston. He drove fast with steady concentration and reached the town in good time. He bought the replacement stores, made a call at the bank and arranged for more funds to be sent from England and lodged in both his name and Shelley's. He was very proud of the way his daughter had adapted to the unbelievably tough camp life and he wanted her to have some private funds of her own when this job was over.

He decided to call in at the hotel and have a light lunch and a long, cool drink. Afterwards he couldn't remember who had been more surprised — Desmond Corby or himself, as they bumped into each other in the hotel lobby.

'Well, you're a long way from camp,' Corby exclaimed.

'I was fetching some stores,' Tom said.

'Same here,' Corby said, edging past him and beginning to walk to the hotel door.

'Let me buy you a drink?' Tom offered. He didn't care much for the man, but he was curious about him and his method of working.

'Another time perhaps, I'm a bit late on my schedule,' Corby said, opening the door and disappearing into the sunshine.

Tom stood for a moment staring at the closed door. He was pretty certain Corby had been on his way into the bar for a drink. He also had the distinct impression that Corby had been embarrassed at seeing him and couldn't wait to get away. Why?

Tom arrived back at Whangiehill to find a super meal waiting for him — steak, as there can only be in Australia, with heaps of vegetables and potatoes in jackets.

'This is a joint effort,' Lisa told him.

'We have been swapping recipes,' Shelley said.

'And talking about their beauty routines practically the whole day,' Neal said with disgust.

'What a bore,' Tom grinned at the boy.

'At least we've been given a good meal, that's something,' Neal said.

'Typical male, even at his age,' Kim said dryly.

If only Chet had been fit and well it would have been a wonderful evening. Shelley seemed to fit into the Donnelly family with ease, and the banter over the meal was good-natured and affectionate.

Desmond Corby arrived later while Tom was sitting with Chet. He came along the passage and looked into the bedroom.

'Still off duty I see. Drilling operations gone dry?' he said to Tom.

'Off duty,' Tom's reply was terse.

'So you haven't had any luck either on this God-forsaken property. This place is the most wretched wasteland I've ever come across.'

Tom moved from his chair swiftly, hoping that the significance of Corby's words hadn't got through to Chet.

'Like some beer?' he asked and began to walk in the direction of the kitchen, forcing Corby to move away from Chet's door.

'Might as well,' the geologist sauntered along the passage.

However, once he reached the kitchen where Lisa and Shelley were tidying up, he assumed his debonair charm for their benefit. Unable to conceal his dislike, Tom returned to Chet's room. The old man had begun to respond to Tom's chat earlier, but now he was fast asleep. Tom had no idea whether he'd heard Corby or not.

He and Shelley left soon after. Corby had looked pleased when they said they were leaving, no doubt hoping to have some time on his own with Lisa. However, she said she was going to bed immediately as she was flaked out. It was easy to see that the extra burden of her father's illness was taking its toll.

It was past midnight when Tom and his daughter reached camp. He was surprised to see lamps burning in the tents.

'You're up late,' he said when Mike came over to the supplies tent.

'No point in trying to sleep when you come into camp making that racket,' Mike snapped.

Tom was astonished; it was so out of character for Mike to be bad-tempered.

'Anything wrong?'

'Not now if we can get some sleep,' Mike stomped off to the tent he shared with Tom.

A few moments later, Shelley brought Tom a mug of tea. He'd almost finished stacking the fresh supplies.

'Here, I expect you could do with this. I was as quiet as possible,' she whispered.

'I expect Mike's had a rough day,' he answered her in soft tones.

It was almost sun-up when Tom woke — in agony. Stomach cramps were attacking his body every few minutes. Sweat broke out on his forehead and for an awful moment he wondered if he was having another long-term ill-effect of his coma. He needed air and he groped his way past the tent flaps, vaguely aware that Mike's camp bed was empty. Outside, he heard someone retching violently. So he wasn't the only one who was ill!

It was later in the morning before the whole crew was fit enough to assemble in the mess tent. Everyone had been ill.

'Apologies for last night,' Mike said at once to Tom. 'I was feeling rough then and I guess I took it out on you.'

'Looks as if we've had food poisoning. I suppose food goes off in this heat.'

Mike shook his head. 'No, I don't think it was the food, Shelley is particularly careful. Also, you and Shelley were away all day yesterday. The boys and I began to feel ill around midnight. You and Shelley weren't sick until sun-up this morning. Shelley says you had tea when you came back last night, so I reckon it's the water.'

'You mean the water tank could be polluted?' Tom asked.

'It can happen easily out here,' Mike said. 'We could have a dead bat or a rodent in the tank. We'll have to flush it out.'

'We'll lose a lot of water that way,' Barry pointed out.

'Sure we will, and we'll be down to our last reserve tank, but we have no option. This means our drinking water will be rationed in the meantime,' Mike announced.

Tom looked round the table at the three men and his daughter. They were all pale and drawn and he knew he looked just as bad.

'We're all going to have a day's rest,' he said.

'We're behind schedule as it is,' Mike began.

'You are all more important to me than finding water,' he said briefly. 'Everyone back to bed for a few hours,' he ordered.

It was late afternoon before the crew assembled to work again. Even then, it took some time to get things under way. Everyone was still weak and lethargic. Tom had started work first as he still intended to pay an evening visit to the homestead. He was worried in case Chet had heard Corby's remarks. The effect on the old man could cause a set-back, at least.

However, Chet seemed a little improved when he spoke to him later. He made no mention of the illness at camp to Lisa or her father. Corby didn't appear at all during the evening, much to Tom's relief.

Next morning, Tom woke before his alarm went off. He lay quite still for a moment, sensing something was wrong. He tried to concentrate, determined to shut out any distractions. Then it hit him — there were no distractions, no noise at all. Total silence hung over the small camp. That was what was wrong — the generator was silent.

Two hours later it was still silent.

'I've found the fault at last,' Rob said. 'It'll take me at least another couple of hours to fix it.'

'We'll rig up a shade for you,' Mike said. 'It's going to be hotter than ever today.'

There was no way they could hurry the repair. Rob was an expert mechanic and knew exactly what he was doing.

Without the generator to provide power they couldn't work, the drill was useless, and the pump. Shelley was having to use some of their precious gas cylinders to cook.

Mike was at a low ebb. 'At times like this you begin to wonder what else can go wrong. We've so little time left. All it needs now is for the drill to pack up.'

'They do say bad luck goes in threes,' Shelley said. 'And, if so, we've had our share now.'

Mike dragged himself out of his depression and raised a smile for Shelley.

'Wish I was superstitious,' he said.

'Walk a way with me, Tom,' he said when Shelley had gone to wash the dishes. 'All this inactivity is giving me too much time to think.'

'About what?'

'Desmond Corby.'

'I know I've gone on a bit about him, but that's only because I can't stand him personally,' Tom said.

'No, there's more than that, Tom.

There's something about him and his way of working that puzzles me.'

'You mean his surveys?'

Mike nodded. 'Now take this rock outcrop here. I'm no geologist, so I can't say for sure, but this might be pre-Cambrian rock.'

'Meaning?'

'Gold has been found in pre-Cambrian rock in several States.'

'You don't think — '

'No, probably there's no gold here, but there could be — must be — some minerals under that pile of rock, yet he hasn't even approached us. He has just as much right to test drill here as we have. It could be in Lisa's interests, too, if we don't find the river.'

Mike and Tom were now privately of the opinion that only a river could keep Whangiehill as a viable cattle station.

Tom suddenly saw what Mike was getting at.

'Do you think we should check him out?'

Mike nodded. 'It occurred to me that

perhaps our friend Norrie Hampson in Sydney could make enquiries about the company Corby works for.'

'Are you sure this is necessary?' Tom was feeling guilty in case his dislike of Corby, which he knew was partly founded on jealousy, could have influenced Mike.

'I don't think he's playing fair with Lisa and Chet,' Mike said flatly.

That did it; anything that affected Lisa was Tom's primary concern.

'I'll write to Norrie now,' he said to Mike.

★ ★ ★

At the homestead that evening, Tom handed Lisa his letter to Norrie.

'Could you give that to the mail man for me, please? I want to keep in touch with Norrie in case he has more contracts for Mike.'

He saw Corby glance quickly at him, but he kept his expression bland. Anyway, it was a partial truth about the letter since he had mentioned that point, although the rest of the letter was a request for detailed information on Corby and his company. But with Corby's next words he realized he'd left it too late.

'Giving up too, are you? I've only three more days to go here,' Corby said.

Tom looked at him blankly, trying to hide the apprehension growing in his heart.

'The company withdraws its offer in three days' time, unless of course, Chet and Lisa accept,' Corby went on. He turned to Lisa. 'Only three days left in which to make up your mind, on both my offers.'

Lisa's face was perfectly still, giving nothing away, but it didn't take much guessing on Tom's part to imagine Corby's other offer.

Chet was more cheerful that evening and had even taken some food. Tom hadn't the heart to tell him about all the bad luck and delays they'd experienced at camp. His own optimism was beginning to falter in the face of their lack of progress and he couldn't bear to think what would happen to Chet if there was only bad news to come.

Lisa walked out to the truck with him when it was time to leave.

'Desmond's company has reduced the amount of the offer,' she said in a low voice. 'They say Whangiehill is poor property and it isn't worth much investment. I haven't had the heart to tell dad yet.'

Tom gritted his teeth. 'Don't tell him yet, Lisa. But you can tell Corby something from me. I never give up!'

They were fighting words, brave yet foolish words, Tom realized as he drove back to camp. Words, too, totally without foundation. He would have to give up if Lisa and Chet accepted Corby's offer.

He couldn't sleep that night at all, worrying about the whole situation, how he'd failed Lisa. If only they hadn't had that run of bad luck! Even Corby didn't have good news for Lisa. Then

Mike's comments about the pre-Cambrian rocks came back to Tom. Maybe the rocks at this site weren't pre-Cambrian, yet surely they were worth surveying? Just exactly where had Corby been surveying, anyway? No one seemed to know. How could the company state that there were few minerals on Whangiehill if the *whole* property hadn't been surveyed?

Tom threw back the sheet covering him and quietly moved out of the tent. Mike was deep in sleep. Outside, Tom stood in the shadow of the tent, looking at the sky, knowing that somewhere in his mind an important fact was eluding him.

There was a rattle of stones, as if some night animal was scrabbling over the rocks. Tom turned his head, thinking of the possible intruder to the mess tent a few nights ago.

Clearly outlined against the moonlight night was the figure of a man, moving towards the pump in a crouching, stealthy way. He lifted his hand as he neared the pump and Tom could just see that he was carrying a long object. For a second the moon caught a reflection on the object and Tom realized it was a metal wrench.

Without a second thought, he launched himself towards that creeping figure.

8

Tom was wearing soft soled casual boots instead of his usual tough leather ones, and so he made little noise as he scrambled over the rocks towards the intruder.

The man was already raising the wrench to attack the pump when Tom came up behind him. He knew nothing until Tom grabbed the upraised arm.

Tom had been relying on the element of surprise to disarm the man, but his plan misfired. The intruder lost his balance and fell heavily against Tom, knocking him to the ground.

He tried to roll over to free his hands but as he did so the man swung the wrench towards him and Tom saw the vicious dull gleam as it descended. He turned and twisted to escape the blow but he was pinned down. Split second thoughts flashed through his brain. No one knew he was here, no one knew about the intruder. He should have called for help. He opened his mouth to shout but it was too late. The wrench struck the back of his head and blackness enveloped him.

★   ★   ★

He guessed he was in a hospital; it wasn't difficult to deduce that. After all, he'd had lots of experience. Yet he wasn't interested in which hospital, where it was; he didn't want to open his eyes; he was afraid to discover how long he'd been here, how much of his life he'd missed this time. He drifted in and out of half sleep, but still refused to open his eyes. To open his eyes would mean having to face the reality of his life now.

This time there was no loss of memory, which might have been a blessing. This time he could remember everything clearly, too clearly; the failure to save Whangiehill, the loss of

Lisa in all probability and the knowledge that he'd put Shelley through a grilling time — all for nothing. It was agony to think what might have happened to Chet.

Even though he fought the periods of consciousness they increased and once or twice he heard the murmurs of the nursing staff as they changed the drip feed in his arm.

Then there was another voice, speaking quietly close to his ear.

'Tom, can you hear me? Please try to hear me. I'm trying to reach you.'

There was something about that voice which was intriguing, begüiling and just when he wanted to stay awake to listen, sleep overtook him again.

He wasn't sure if he was dreaming or not when he heard the voice again some time later.

'Tom, please wake up, please give me a sign that you can hear me. It's Lisa. I'm still here, Tom.'

Tom lay perfectly still, afraid to stir in case that tender voice should disappear.

'Tom,' Lisa went on. 'There are so many things I should have said to you. You've come to mean so much to us all at Whangiehill, and I think we just all took you for granted. We all miss you so much. Everybody cares so much,' her voice faded to a whisper and he had to strain to hear the next words. 'I care, Tom . . . so much. I didn't know until this happened. Please, Tom, get well, I can't . . . go on without you . . . '

He heard some rustling movements and then the sound of a door closing very quietly. He waited a few more moments, then carefully opened his eyes.

He was alone in a small room, painted in pale duck egg blue. There was his bed, a locker, two chairs. A Venetian blind, closed, covered the window.

Everything was a little spartan looking, and then he realized there were no flowers in the room, no fruit. The only indication of a patient in his room was himself, lying motionless on the bed, a drip feed connected to his left arm. Had he been here so long that flowers had died, fruit had rotted?

Yet Tom had noted all the details in a detached way because his mind was filled with Lisa's words, filled and overflowing with wonder at her words, at the fact that she cared. She'd lost Whangiehill and yet she still cared.

This was so different from his return to life last year. Then he'd lost someone he cared for; this time he'd found someone.

For a moment he wanted to summon a nurse to find Lisa and bring her back, to tell her he'd heard what she said and that he loved her, too. For a moment, that was what he wanted to do.

But now his eyes were open and he faced reality. He faced the fact that he was once again in a hospital, having had another blow to his already weakened body. How much could his body take? How much of a man was he now? How could he tell a young woman like Lisa that he loved her and bind her to him?

She deserved a young, healthy man, not an old crock.

He moved his fingers around the bed and found a buzzer attached to a cord. He pressed the buzzer. Within a few minutes, a nurse arrived.

'Mr Price! You're awake, how marvellous! How are you feeling?'

Expertly she took his pulse, while smiling encouragingly at him.

'What a pity, your visitor has just left. She's hardly left your bedside, too. We shall have to telephone her with the good news.'

After making a few more routine checks, the nurse left him.

He was determined to stay awake, determined to recover as quickly as possible. He must get himself fit and make a new life with Shelley. He had to get out of Lisa's life, he wasn't the man for her. He would pretend he'd just come round when next he saw her. He would never let her know he'd heard her words today. Future conversation with her would be friendly, but never on a personal plane, never allowing her to tell him of her feelings. After he'd left the Outback, she'd soon forget him.

It was a difficult plan to carry out, especially once he saw her again next day. She'd never looked so beautiful to him. She was wearing a plain green cotton skirt, with a white blouse, patterned with a green leaf design. She looked far too fragile to survive in the Outback.

'Hello, Tom,' she smiled shyly at him from the doorway of the room. 'I'm . . . we're all so glad you're going to be okay. Everyone sends their love,' she advanced towards the bed, her arms laden with parcels.

The closer she came to him, the weaker became Tom's resolve. He wanted to stretch out to her, to hold her hand, to hear again those words she'd whispered to him yesterday.

Lisa busied herself stacking the parcels on his locker.

'May I unpack these for you? I don't know what you're going to do with them all,' she was speaking quickly, jerkily, and he realized that she was self-conscious, too.

'Desmond Corby is in this hospital, too,' she said.

'It was Desmond at the pump then?' Tom asked, for a fleeting second thinking it incongruous that these should be his first words to the woman he loved.

She nodded. 'The mineral company did want Whangiehill, but at a low price. Desmond was sent to survey it, not properly, no real deep bores in case he found something worthwhile and we found out about it. He only found surface lodes because he only surveyed the surface. The company was out to cheat us of our rights.'

She began to unwrap a parcel.

'They would have succeeded, too, if you hadn't been there, Tom. If you hadn't come back to drill for water, we'd have taken Desmond and his company at face value.'

Tom said nothing for a moment.

Corby and his company had done considerable damage to a number of people.

'Lisa, I have to know about Chet,' he said.

To his immense relief, her face lit up.

'In the saddle again, poking his nose in everywhere, making a nuisance of himself,' she told him, laughing. 'Isn't that marvellous?'

She saw the question in his eyes.

'When he heard what had happened to you, he got himself well mighty quick. You were right, Tom, he was giving up. But he got so mad that you'd been hurt on account of us, that he began eating, getting up and around and he took your place at the drilling rig.'

'Are they still all there?' he asked.

She hesitated for a moment, then said: 'Yes, the team is working on. They're working from the homestead now. Shelley is there, looking after Kim and Neal for me, but everything is going well now.'

Tom looked away. If they were still working that meant they hadn't found the river. How long had it been now?

'You know, Desmond claims he didn't mean to hurt you,' Lisa said. 'He said you pulled him down and the wrench hit you by mistake.'

Tom could vividly remember the gleam on the wrench as it had been swung towards him. That was no accident.

'He was acting on his own at your site,' she went on. 'He had no instructions from the company to damage your workings.'

Did she still have some feelings for the man, Tom wondered, that she should defend him so? But Lisa soon put him clear on that point.

'I can't believe anyone could act the way he did,' she said. 'Oh, I knew he was a smoothie from the moment I met him, but I didn't think he would do anything criminal. To think I gave him house room,' she looked apologetically at Tom. 'I tried hard to be nice, not to antagonize him, in case we had to take his company's money in the end. I feel terrible about that now.'

'It's all right, Lisa, I understand, you were in a rotten position.'

For a moment she just looked at him and he saw her face soften and her eyes smile at him. He knew instinctively she was going to tell him of her feelings for him.

'What's in all those parcels, then?' he asked quickly.

The light went out of her eyes and she turned to the locker. There was a luscious cake from Shelley, some oddly shaped biscuits from Kim with a note to say that she was just an apprentice cook, and a carved horse from Neal, all his own work, too.

Then Lisa handed him a bottle of clear liquid.

'From Mike,' she said.

Tom stared at it. It certainly wasn't whisky or brandy, it was too colourless.

'Gin?' he asked her.

She laughed and shook her head.

Gently she took the bottle from him and unscrewed the top.

'Smell,' she held the bottle under his nose.

'Nothing,' he looked at her, puzzled.

'Not spirits, just pure clear water. It's free from chemicals, our own drinking water.'

It still took a few more moments for the significance to sink in.

Then the words came out haltingly. 'We have found a source of pure drinking water at Whangiehill?'

She just smiled at him, her eyes glad, yet tender.

'I've had it analysed here in Gillieston; it's quite pure.'

Gradually he took in the full meaning of her statement.

'You mean, this hospital is in Gillieston — not Sydney?'

'Of course it's Gillieston hospital. There was no need to take you all the way to Sydney. You'll be better in a few days. The dressing will be off soon, the doctor says.'

Slowly Tom raised his right hand to his head. Sure enough, there was a large pad at the back of his head.

'Does this mean I was just knocked out, I haven't been in another coma?'

'You've been out cold for three days, Tom, and I . . . we've been worried sick about you, but no, you haven't been in a coma.'

The door swung open and a nurse entered briskly.

'Time's up, I'm afraid, Mrs Donnelly. Mr Price must have some more rest.'

'Yes, of course,' Lisa jumped up from her chair. 'Goodbye for now, Tom. I'll be back soon,' she finished softly.

'Lisa — ,' he reached out to her. There was so much he wanted to say to her now he knew he hadn't been in a coma. Now that he knew he'd only had a bang on the head. That was nothing much; he wasn't back to the beginning as he had been in England last time.

'You'll have plenty of time to chat on the next visit,' the nurse said firmly, pointedly holding open the door for Lisa.

Lisa smiled at him from the door and then was gone.

*   *   *

Shelley was actually his next visitor the following day.

'Hi, Dad, am I glad this is not a re-run of last time,' she dropped down into the chair beside his bed, after giving him a warm kiss. 'Still, I've loads of sympathy, you've been pretty crook.'

'It didn't take you long to pick up some Australian slang,' he grinned at her.

She blushed a little. 'It must be the company I keep.'

He smiled at her. 'I have no objections.' It was true, he admired Mike Yarrow tremendously.

'Good on you,' she gave him another example of slang. 'Listen, Dad, I've been making pretty free with your money.'

243

'That's what it's for,' he told her, remembering he'd deposited money in her name just before Desmond's attack. Fate must have been on his side for part of that day, anyway.

'After we had you flown out to hospital from the site,' she told him. 'I began to pack up camp, then Mike stopped me.'

' 'Do you think we should just sit around on our backsides while your dad is in hospital, Shelley?' he said. 'Don't you think we should carry on here, that's what Tom would expect us to do.''

'Of course, I got really mad with him. There I was, worried out of my mind about you, especially remembering what had happened to you before, and he wanted me to carry on working!'

Tom smiled at her.

'Yes, Dad, you're right,' she said. 'It was the best thing for me. So I came into Gillieston to see if I could raise some money and found that I had acquired a substantial bank account.

You old sly boots, you never said a thing.'

'I didn't have time.'

'Anyway, I've taken out quite a bit of cash. We paid Rob and Barry since the first month's contract was completed, but they said they'd like to carry on until the job was finished.' She hesitated. 'Mike's gone back to the first location chosen by Chet.'

'You mean he didn't find anything at the original creek source in the rocks?'

'What's that?' Shelley pointed to the bottle of pure water, still sitting atop Tom's locker. 'And what's better than one source of water? Two', she said succinctly.

'Shelley, take me through this slowly,' he said. 'Is Whangiehill going to be a viable station again?'

She looked away from him and shrugged. 'If we can find water at the original location, it should be. After all, the drought can't last forever, can it?'

Tom thought that a rather evasive answer. He and Mike had felt that only a proper river could save the station. Now, if they were thinking of another source and being optimistic about the end of the drought, they were pinning their hopes on something quite different.

'I haven't told Mummy what happened to you,' Shelley said. 'I thought maybe you wouldn't want to worry her again.'

'No, I wouldn't, that was the right decision, Shelley. She would only have felt guilty and after all it had nothing to do with her.'

'She sent you a letter,' her voice was offhand as she handed him an envelope. 'I had one, too.'

Tom guessed the contents right away from Shelley's manner.

'She's put the divorce in motion?'

His daughter nodded, watching him closely.

'It's okay now, isn't it, Dad?'

'Yes, it's okay now. I'll always have regrets about what happened, but I have found a new life and I'm happy.'

She took his hand. 'Yes, I guessed you were. And so am I.'

'I've been worried about that, my dear,' he said to her. 'Dumping you down here in the middle of this vast continent, seeing you work all hours of the day until you're dropping, I've been thinking that I've been so selfish, that I've ruined your life.'

'No, Dad, it's just the opposite. Mind you, if someone had told me two months ago in England that I'd be sleeping in a tent, cooking in the open, forgetting what lipsticks and hairdos were, I'd have said they'd gone bananas,' she laughed, then spoke more quietly. 'It sounds a bit square, but I think I've found myself here. I can't ever imagine myself back in a social whirl with the tennis crowd, and hacking with the girls at the riding stables, and worrying whether I'll be ostracized if I wear ankle boots instead of knee-length ones. These things don't matter in real life, do they? And here — the Outback, Whangiehill, that's real life. And I've met some wonderful people, made some good friends, friends that really matter to me.'

'I'm glad,' said Tom. 'You see, I've made a commitment to Whangiehill and I want to stand by that whether the station collapses or survives.'

'Sure, Dad, I know. And I'm with you all the way. Say, you haven't been lying here worrying about me on top of everything else? You know I would have come to hospital to see you before, but to tell the truth, I thought Lisa should be the one with you. She's been nearly out of her mind with worry and I sort of thought you'd like to see her first, too.'

Shelley's tone had been airy, but Tom saw her giving him a very straight look. He said nothing.

She grinned at him. 'Okay, play it cool, but I'm glad about Lisa, too.'

Lisa came in after Shelley had gone, but Tom sensed a wariness in her immediately. He knew at once it was because he had stopped her confessing her feelings for him on her last visit. How he wished he could have that afternoon over again. He'd spoken of so many other things, when all the time all that mattered was each other.

Somehow, though, it was impossible to recapture the mood of that special time. It frightened him that perhaps they never would. Maybe, too, Lisa just thought she was in love with him since he'd been a bit of a hero over Desmond. Perhaps once she saw him back at Whangiehill, she'd realize her mistake.

Within a few days Tom was up and about in the hospital. The doctor had told him that he'd be back to normal with a few days' rest and that no permanent damage had been done. As far as he could tell, Tom had completely recovered from the coma, too.

Tom was sitting in the day room of the ward when Norrie Hampson walked in.

'Well, sport, you're a glutton for punishment, aren't you?' he greeted Tom.

'What on earth are you doing out here?' Tom was astonished to see his friend so far from Sydney.

'Shelley got a message to me that you'd been playing the hero, like, and I came out to see if she was telling the truth.'

Tom smiled at his friend, knowing Norrie's casual talk hid real concern.

'A personal call to the hospital by telephone would have been cheaper,' he joked.

'True, still I was curious to see what had brought you — and kept you — in the Outback.'

'A stupid, crazy dream, I suppose,' Tom said despondently. 'I should have accepted that I didn't know this country, didn't know the power of Nature here. I guess I raised false hopes.'

'The job in Canberra would have been child's play compared to this,' Norrie said. 'Yet it wouldn't have been a challenge to you, and that's what Australia is all about, mate, as you've discovered the hard way. A lot of people are taking off their hats to you on account of your guts and determination to succeed.'

Tom looked at Norrie in amazement; he was sure everyone would think he'd been foolhardy.

'I'll stop now, before the hankies come out,' Norrie grinned. 'I've had a good look at Whangiehill, there's a great deal of potential there to make it a better cattle station.'

Tom looked sceptical.

Norrie changed the subject quickly.

'I've been having a word with Mike, too. Heard about a consultancy coming up in his line and I reckon he's the man for the job.'

'What does Mike think?' Tom asked.

'He's interested, but he won't commit himself yet.'

'He's determined to finish the job at Whangiehill, isn't he?' Tom said. 'I'd hate him to lose a good job on my account.'

'He won't,' Norrie was brief. 'By the

way, I got your letter about Corby. I wish I'd known earlier that he and his company were surveying at Whangie-hill. Their operations have always been a bit shady, though I've never known them to resort to violence before.'

'He's passing it off as an accident,' Tom said.

Norrie looked at him closely. 'M'm, I didn't think it was, even though Corby said he broke his leg in the fall. As there were no witnesses though, you have no proof.'

'That's true,' Tom agreed. 'I'd hate to think he'd get away with it again.'

'He won't, we've passed the word around. He and his company are finished. Still, Lisa's feeling pretty low about what happened to you.'

'It wasn't her fault, we all trusted him and at one time I even thought she was fond of him.'

'She is too sensible to be taken in by anyone as obvious as him. She told me all about him. It's obvious he only suggested marriage to her in order to detract attention from his devious plans,' Norrie grinned at him. 'No, that lady knows where her heart belongs.'

Tom said nothing, but suspected that his feelings were evident to Norrie.

Norrie wagged a finger at Tom. 'Lisa is one very special lady and don't you overlook that!'

That special lady came to fetch him home from hospital a few days later. Tom felt fine and was anxious to be at Whangiehill to see what, if anything, could be done to save the station.

He'd been unable to elicit information from any of his visitors, they all shied away from the subject of the cattle. He surmised they were anxious not to upset him by giving him additional worries.

He and Lisa chatted occasionally on the drive from Gillieston. Once through the perimeter fence gate to Whangiehill, Tom began to feel anxiety knots in his stomach, yet nothing had changed.

Still the sun shone down from an empty sky onto the empty land; only their truck with its trailing cloud of red dust, moved in the landscape.

The vegetation was as parched as ever, the odd trees they passed stood like carved sentinels, holding out bare branches like stiff arms. This was Whangiehill; this was the Outback.

After a while the homestead came in sight and, as they drew nearer, Tom could see figures on the verandah. Lisa and he drew up to a right royal welcome.

Tom jumped down from the truck and was soon shaking hands and kissing people at the same time. He was very touched at the welcome. Everyone was there, including Banka and the drillers. He tried to hide a sneaking feeling of despondency. Since the drillers were there, no one was working. Had they given up?

A glass of cool beer was put in his hand and he found himself being ushered along the verandah to the back of the house. There, a table had been laid with food and more drinks. Tom was surprised, the heat was stifling and they usually ate indoors at this time of day.

'Sit down, sit down,' Chet, looking younger and fitter than before, guided Tom towards a chair.

'Wait a minute, Tom,' Neal yelled suddenly. 'Some careless person has left binoculars on your chair.'

Tom laughed at Neal's out of character formal remark. As he sat down, Neal handed him the binoculars.

'I've been tracking a joey this morning, you can still see him out there — look!'

Tom lifted the binoculars to his eyes to search out the kangaroo. Although he could make out a vague shape, he had to sharpen the focus.

'I hate to disappoint you, Neal, but that isn't a — ' Tom adjusted the focus again. There was more than one shape out there — three, four, no more, kept slowly moving into his line of vision. They were the wrong shape for kangaroos and those animals were grazing!

Tom lowered the glasses and looked around at everyone. Triumphant knowing grins and smiles met his eyes.

At once Tom lifted the glasses again and looked at those distant shapes. They were grazing just below the Whangie Hill itself.

'Tom, we have a creek again, a real creek of water at Whangiehill,' Neal burst out, unable to hold the secret a second longer.

Then everyone was moving towards Tom again, slapping him on the back, pumping his hand.

'We found the river,' Mike shouted above the hubbub.

'Our cattle are grazing again at Whangiehill,' Chet's voice was thick with emotion and pride.

'Look again, Dad, and see what Banka has been doing,' Shelley said.

Tom inspected the land closely. Banka had been digging a new course for the water to take; one that would lead it right to the homestead.

'We're controlling the flow at the

moment,' Mike explained. 'Until new storage tanks are built at the homestead here.'

'Uncle Norrie says that if you want a swimming pool here, he'll build it, Tom,' Neal chipped in.

'Trust him,' Tom laughed. Then he had to sit down. This had all been a bit of a shock to him. He realized they'd all planned it as a wonderful surprise, but if only they knew how despondent he'd been thinking things had gone the other way. However, no one must ever know that.

It took some time for everyone to settle down again and to eat the celebration feast which Lisa and Shelley had prepared.

'We hit the big gusher the day after you were hurt,' Mike told him. 'If we hadn't been delayed by Corby's mischief we'd have discovered it earlier and you would have been okay.'

'You mean all our little misfortunes were his work?' Tom asked.

Mike sighed. 'Yeah, I'd had my

suspicions about him from the very beginning. I knew no animal could have toppled the shelves in the mess tent.'

'He threw a dead bat into the water tank,' Shelley told Tom, with disgust.

'He knew what he was doing when he stopped the generator,' Rob said. 'That's why it took me so long to repair. If he'd managed to wreck the pump, it would have taken us days, even weeks, to get a replacement out to Whangiehill.'

'But he reckoned without Superman Tom,' Shelley leaned over and kissed Tom.

'Yeah, you're something special,' Neal said. 'When you first came out here and you couldn't ride I was really worried for you. I mean, everyone knows how to — '

Suddenly Kim grabbed Neal by the neck of his shirt and yanked him away from Tom.

'I'm so glad you're home, Tom. You'll have to take Neal in hand again, he's an objectionable child,' Kim said.

For a moment, Tom held his breath. Kim had said 'home'. Did that mean they wanted him to stay? Lisa was standing by the verandah rail but he couldn't bring himself to look at her, not in front of everyone.

'You haven't changed your mind about being part owner of Whangiehill, Tom?' Chet asked, quietly drawing him away from the others.

'Not if you still want me,' Tom said.

'Sure do, we're really proud to have you here,' Suddenly Chet smiled and he looked about twenty years younger. 'There's another secret we've been saving up for you. Mike and I found water at my original location.'

'Say, Chet, that's fantastic!' Tom said.

Mike joined them.

'Two sources of irrigation on one station is every cattle owner's dream,' Mike said. 'Now the herd can be increased.'

'You've done a great job all round, Mike,' Tom said appreciatively.

'It's had a good spin-off for me.

Norrie reckons that I could get that consultancy job.'

'Is that what you want?'

Mike nodded. 'It means I can have a home base and be able to spend most of my time there. I wouldn't need to be at a potential well for weeks on end, such as here. I could fly out to various rigs just for a few days, to advise. I could have a real home life, something to offer someone.'

From Mike's direct look, Tom guessed he had someone in mind and suspected it was Shelley. He glanced across the room to where his daughter was helping Lisa. She was still very young, but had matured tremendously in the few short weeks she'd been in Australia and besides he knew she liked the life here. If she truly loved Mike, he'd have no objection.

There was only one person with whom he hadn't been able to talk since he'd arrived back at Whangiehill and that was Lisa. He'd seen tears of joy in her eyes when he'd first spotted the cattle at the creek and he'd wanted to reach out to her then, but what he had to say was only for her ears.

At last everyone went to bed, but Tom knew where to find Lisa. She was sitting on the verandah rail, leaning against an upright post, gazing out at the empty night sky.

Tom went over to her and leant on the rail.

'You did it all for Chet, and the children and me, didn't you?' she said.

'Yes.'

'To pay off a debt you felt you owed?'

'No. Only because I care. Because I love you, and the children and Chet, but most of all you, my dear.'

Lisa was still staring out at the sky.

'Can you hear me now, Tom?' she asked quietly.

He knew then that she guessed he'd heard her whispered words at his bedside in the hospital.

'I didn't know at the time whether I deserved those words or not.'

'I meant them no matter what

happened here,' she turned to him then and he saw the love and honesty in her eyes.

He took her in his arms and there was no need for further words. He knew they would be together forever once he was free. As he bent to kiss her there was a sudden splash as a night animal stumbled on the new flow of water.

Startled, they drew apart for a moment, then began laughing and hugging each other.

That splash was the loveliest sound in the world to them.

THE END

THE DOCTOR WAS A DOLL

Claire Vernon

Jackie runs a riding-school and, living happily with her father, feels no desire to get married. When Dr. Simon Hanson comes to the town, Jackie's friends try to matchmake, but he, like Jackie, wishes to remain single and they become good friends. When Jackie's father decides to remarry, she feels she is left all alone, not knowing the happiness that is waiting around the corner.

TO BE WITH YOU

Audrey Weigh

Heather, the proud owner of a small bus line, loves the countryside in her corner of Tasmania. Her life begins to change when two new men move into the area. Colin's charm overcomes her first resistance, while Grant also proves a warmer person than expected. But Colin is jealous when Grant gains special attention. The final test comes with the prospect of living in Hobart. Could Heather bear to leave her home and her business to be with the man she loves?